THE OFFICIAL MOVIE NOVELIZATION

RETURN OF XANDER CAGE

NOVELIZATION BY TIM WAGGONER
BASED ON THE MOTION PICTURE
WRITTEN BY F. SCOTT FRAZIER
BASED ON THE CHARACTERS CREATED BY RICH WILKES
DIRECTED BY D.J. CARUSO

TITAN BOOKS

xXx: Return of Xander Cage
Print edition ISBN: 9781785655142
E-book edition ISBN: 9781785655159

Published by Titan Books
A division of Titan Publishing Group Ltd
144 Southwark Street, London SE1 0UP

First edition: January 2017
1 3 5 7 9 10 8 6 4 2

A CIP catalogue record for this title is available from the British Library.

Printed and bound by CPI Group (UK) Ltd, Croydon, CR0 4YY

Did you enjoy this book? We love to hear from our readers. Please
email us at readerfeedback@titanemail.com or write to us at Reader
Feedback at the above address.

To receive advance information, news, competitions, and exclusive
offers online, please sign up for the Titan newsletter on our website:
www.titanbooks.com

RETURN OF XANDER CAGE

THIS ONE'S FOR JONATHAN MABERRY

—WRITER, TEACHER, FRIEND.

Sputnik 1, *the first artificial satellite to orbit the Earth, was launched by the Soviet Union in 1957. It was about the size of a beach ball, weighed only 183.9 pounds, and took 98 minutes to orbit the globe. Today there are approximately 1,490 active satellites in orbit, and 2,691 inactive, all traveling at least 17,000 miles per hour. The largest satellites are big as a school bus and weigh up to 6 tons, while the smallest weigh as little as 2.2 pounds. Altitude for satellites varies depending on type. They can orbit as low as 100 miles above the Earth's surface or as high as 50,000 miles. They are owned by governments large and small, as well as private companies. There are hamsats, navsats, weather sats, photo sats, science sats, communication and broadcast sats, military comsats, and—of course—spysats. Some remain in geostationary orbit, others orbit the planet in circular or elliptical patterns, and some can move from one place to another as necessary.*

Basically, there's a shitload of metal whizzing above us that we are completely unaware of, but which makes our tech-obsessed lifestyles possible. An intricate web of hardware and software representing the pinnacle of human scientific achievement. But when satellite orbits decay—as they eventually do—machines that cost between 50 and 400 million dollars to build and launch become useless junk plummeting back toward the planet that sent them up in the first place. One hundred tons of space debris fall every year—but there's no reason to lose your shit about it. Most of it burns up on reentry, but even if some material survives this atmospheric cremation, the odds of it hitting a particular individual—like you—is one in twenty trillion. Damn good odds, right?

But what if someone found a way to change those odds?

Augustus Gibbons stood at the counter of the Dumpling Palace, waiting for the owner to finish preparing his order. Normally, he would've sat at a table and let a waiter bring his food, but this wasn't a normal day. No one else was present. No waiters, no other customers, only Gibbons, the owner, and Gibbons's guest. And it was to this guest that Gibbons spoke.

"You know how I came up with the idea for the Triple-X program? Skateboards and swimming pools.

No shit. True story. Skateboards used to be stuck on the ground, adolescent transportation. But then 1977 happens. Big drought hits Southern California. Got so bad, rich suburbanites couldn't afford to keep their swimming pools filled. And that's when some kid realized he could skate all those empty pools, get some really nasty air. *Dogtown and Z-Boys*. It's a movie. You seen it? Doesn't matter.

"Anyhow, before you know it, our hero was doing things on a board no one had ever seen before. Things the world thought were impossible.

"The kid *needed* those empty pools. That's why Triple-X."

The owner set two plates of steaming food on the counter one at a time, and Gibbons took a deep breath, inhaling the dishes' delicious aromas.

God-DAMN, I love Chinese food! Gibbons thought. One of the perks of his job was that he could choose the places where he conducted business meetings, which meant that he got to visit his favorite bars and restaurants and put the bill on his expense account. That way, if the meeting didn't go so well, at least he got a few good drinks or an excellent meal out of it.

Gibbon carried the two plates of food—which were both hot—back to the table as fast as he could. He set the mixed vegetable stir fry in front of his seat and the chow mein in front of his guest. He then sat down, took a sip of the hot tea he had previously ordered, snatched up his chopsticks and began to eat. A Louis Armstrong tune was playing over the restaurant's sound system, his most famous: "What a Wonderful World."

"'Red roses, too…' I love that song. You know, they say the world's a safer place than it's ever been in the history of civilization. I call bullshit. Sure, there's no dagger-in-the-teeth Kalashnikov-bearing Mongol hordes descending on the Beltway—but honestly, do you feel safer today than you did yesterday? I know I don't. We got the biggest, most expensive military in the world, and we're still scared of shoe and tighty-whitey bombs at the airport. Why is that? Because soldiers are built to take orders and fight wars… But we are not at war; we are at peril. That's why Triple-X."

The Dumpling Palace's décor was a blend of modern and old-fashioned. High windows lined one wall, letting in plenty of light and providing a view of the buildings across the street. Usually the downtown area was busy with pedestrians and traffic, but there weren't any people out right now, not at this hour. The restaurant's more traditional touches included real wooden chopsticks—not the dumbass plastic ones that Gibbons hated—and fake roast ducks hanging in the window. He liked the mix of new and old because he thought of himself in similar terms. He was in his late sixties—hence the old part—but he'd spent his career trying to find new and innovative ways to do his work. He had to if he wanted to keep on saving lives. The bad guys were always looking for new ways to fuck shit up, which meant people like him had to work overtime just to keep up with them.

At this stage in his life, Gibbons liked to dress well, and he paid for his clothes out of his own pocket instead of making taxpayers pick up the tab. In his line of work, you never knew when the Grim Reaper was going to catch up with you, so you might as well be dressed for your funeral, just in case. This day looking good meant wearing a pair of metal-rimmed glasses, a designer regular fit wool suit, and a striped men's skinny tie. A stretch cotton-blend white shirt and Italian-made leather dress shoes completed his look. Total price tag, within spitting distance of $2000 dollars. Expensive, sure— especially on a government salary. But Gibbons figured he'd earned the right to enjoy some of the finer things in life. And it never hurt to look good when making a recruiting speech.

Sitting across the table from Gibbons was a slender, fit man in his twenties. He was dressed more casually than the spymaster—long-sleeved white shirt, dark blue jacket, jeans, white sneakers, and a blue cap he wore backwards. He sported several days' worth of stubble, not so thick it could be called a beard. If Gibbons hadn't rented the entire restaurant for this meeting and there were other customers around, he had no doubt that his guest would be recognized by more than a few of them. Neymar—full name Neymar da Silva Santos Júnior—was one of the most famous soccer players on earth, and in 2016, ESPN had named him the world's fourth most famous athlete overall.

Neymar hadn't touched his food the entire time Gibbons had been giving his sales pitch.

"What's the matter? You on a diet or something? You not hungry? I can get my man Yao back there to hook you up with a broccoli and beef that'll make your balls tingle."

"It's seven-thirty in the morning," Neymar said.

"So? It's lunch or dinnertime somewhere in the world. Come, eat up. You know who does feel safe? The men in charge. The world beaters, the top-shelf, par-excellence, *point*-one-percent, the Ayatollahs With All the Dollahs.

"Because somewhere down the line, those righteous bastards made a deal with the devil, traded liberty for safety and we, we the people, ended up losing both. That's why Triple-X. We put out the fires those bastards profit from. We protect everyone, not just the chosen few. We watch the watchers. We can save the world in ways the world doesn't even realize it needs saving. Everybody else is stuck on the ground. We're doing shit on a board nobody's ever seen before."

Gibbons paused a beat to let it all sink in.

"Well, that's my pitch. Always was a better spy than salesman. So what do you say?"

"You got it all wrong. I'm no hero, just a footballer."

"My bad… I'll stop wasting your time. Whoever said there's no such thing as a free lunch?"

Frustrated, Gibbons stood up and walked to the front counter, intending to pay for their meals—and for the early-morning restaurant rental. *Looks like you're losing your touch, old man,* he thought. There was a time when he could talk a prospective agent into sticking his dick into a meat grinder for dear old Uncle Samuel. But it seemed those days were behind him.

Despite the fact that the Dumpling Palace wasn't officially open yet, a bell tinkled as someone entered. Yao had just walked up to the counter to settle the bill with Gibbons, and now both men looked over to check out the newcomer. But it only took a glance for Gibbons to know the man wasn't here because he had a sudden early-morning craving for moo shu pork. The man wore a dark jacket and a black ski mask, and if the latter hadn't been a tip-off the guy was looking for trouble, the double-barreled shotgun he carried was more than definitive proof. The masked man raised the shotgun as he approached Gibbons and Yao.

"Down on the ground! Empty the register! Hurry up!"

The motherfucker sounded like he meant business, and Yao raised his hands in a show of compliance. But instead of starting to lower himself to the floor, Gibbons glanced at Neymar.

Moving with a fluid speed that was beautiful to watch, Neymar grabbed a metal napkin container from the table at the same time he rose from his seat. He tossed the container in front of him, but before it could hit the ground, he swung his right foot toward it. The kick had so much power behind it that the container became a silver blur as it streaked toward the would-be robber's head. The container slammed into the man's forehead before he could react. There was a sickening sound of metal striking bone, and the container bounced off the man's skull. His eyes rolled white, and he collapsed to the floor, unconscious. The napkin container hit the floor an instant later, bounced a couple times, and then was still.

For a second, neither Gibbons, Neymar, or Yao said anything. They just stared at the masked man, who looked as if he was going to be out cold for a very long time. The man had managed to hold onto the shotgun when he fell, and Gibbons quickly bent down and took it from his hand. Holding the weapon down at his side, he walked back toward Neymar. This was always the hardest part: Gibbons had to maintain a straight face when inside he was grinning from ear to ear. When the speech alone didn't work, a little bit of interactive theater usually did the trick. Of course, Agent Dunlevy was going to have one hell of a headache when he woke up. Who knows? As hard as Reymar kicked, the poor sonofabitch might end up with a concussion. But if Dunlevy's performance helped convince Neymar to join Triple-X, then Gibbons would buy the agent a case of scotch to help soothe his aching head.

"And you say you're no hero. Well, I call bullshit on that, too. You're exactly the kind of hero this world needs. End of the day, it comes down to the same question I've asked my wife every Friday night for the last twenty years. You want some of this, or you just gonna—"

Before Gibbons could finish his sentence, the restaurant erupted in a blast of fire and sound, the explosion so violent, so intense, so all-consuming, that within seconds the restaurant—and a significant portion of the area surrounding it—were reduced to little more than charred rubble and twisted, blackened metal.

If Gibbons had still been present to gaze upon the destruction, his most likely reaction would've been to think, *And I almost had the kid ready to sign on the dotted line, too. Ain't that a pisser?*

1

An SUV slid smooth and silent through the nighttime traffic. New York might've been the city that never sleeps, but the traffic was lighter at night than during the day—if only marginally so—and the driver had no trouble weaving back and forth between lanes to get around slow-moving vehicles. The passenger in the back wasn't worried about the driver getting pulled over by the police for speeding or reckless operation. For one thing, this was Manhattan. If the cops stopped every driver who operated his or her vehicle like a lunatic who'd downed a dozen cans of energy drink in one sitting, they wouldn't have time to scratch their asses, let alone get anything else done. And if by some minor miracle a patrol officer did pull them over, then that overachieving do-gooder would quickly find himself in shit-deep trouble when he learned the man riding in the back was the director of the goddamned CIA.

If anyone had been able to see through the vehicle's tinted windows, they would've seen a man in his fifties, wearing a suit that cost almost as much as the SUV itself. At first glance, he would've seemed calm, almost relaxed. He sat back against the seat, legs crossed, hands resting in his lap. But a closer look would've revealed that his lips were set in a tight line, his eyes were narrowed, and there was a slight furrow in his brow caused half by concern and half by concentration.

There was, to use professional spy jargon, a Situation, which needed the Director's attention ASA-fucking-P. A text, email, or phone call—all double, triple, and quadruple encrypted, of course—wouldn't cut it. No, this shitstorm required he put in a personal appearance. When you were the director of the greatest intelligence-gathering organization on the planet—and to hell with what the Russians and Chinese might say about that claim—sometimes you had to make a house call. So what if he'd had to leave his mistress alone in a hot tub with an unopened bottle of Domaine du Comte Liger-Belair La Romanee Grand Cru—a fine wine that cost almost $3,000 a bottle—sitting on the kitchen counter of her scandalously expensive penthouse apartment, which he paid for, naturally. She'd still be waiting for him when he got back and, more importantly, the wine would keep.

The driver—Carl, the Director thought, but he was terrible at remembering worker-bee names so he wasn't sure—slowed as they drew near a certain skyscraper. Its construction was modern—all gleaming steel and glass panels—but that didn't make it stand out, not in Manhattan where there were so many buildings; it was like new ones popped up like mushrooms every time it rained. It was just another building, one thousands of people passed by day after day, without even giving it a second thought—and that was just the way the Director liked it.

Carl—or whoever—pulled the SUV up to the front of the building, and the Director opened the back passenger door and stepped onto the sidewalk in perfectly polished thousand-dollar loafers. He entered the building's lobby alone. There was a certain amount of risk to traveling like this—only one driver, no guards—but it had its advantage, too. He could make better time without an entourage, and the fewer people he had with him, the less likely he was to draw the media's attention. He was hardly pop-star famous, and the average Jane or Joe on the street would pass him by without recognizing him. But travel with a collection of men and women all wearing the same basic clothes, sporting the same basic haircut, all wearing sunglasses, all on constant lookout for even the hint of a suspicion of an inkling of a threat to their boss, and you risked drawing so many eyes to you that someone was bound to recognize you sooner or later. And what kind of a spymaster would he be if he allowed that to happen when he was working? *Really* working, and not merely posing for the cameras.

The lobby was empty, no security personnel present. No guards were necessary. They'd just be more eyes to see things they shouldn't—and the CIA had put automated security procedures in place that were better than any human could ever hope to be. The Director walked across the lobby. The sound of his loafers was the only noise in the lobby, and he walked until he came to a featureless door in the wall on the far side of the lobby. A keypad was mounted next to the door and the Director entered a long alphanumeric pass code. When he was finished, multiple locks disengaged, and the door slid open. He stepped into a long, narrow hallway and continued walking, the door closing after him automatically.

A beautiful brunette woman dressed in skintight black leather darted down the corridor the Director had just vacated. She moved with astonishing swiftness, but for all her speed her feet made absolutely no noise on the floor. Her goal was to reach the door before it closed and locked, but despite how fast she ran, she knew she wasn't going to make it in time. She gritted her teeth and poured all of her energy into running. And then, when she was within several feet of the door, she slid into splits and her right foot slipped between the door and the jamb at the last possible second. She wasn't sweating or winded from her all-out exertion. She looked as if she'd done nothing more remarkable than get up off the couch and walk into the kitchen to make herself a snack. But there were few people on the planet who could do what Serena just had, and she knew it.

She allowed herself a quick smile. *So far, so good. Now for step two.*

At the end of the hall, the Director came to an elevator door. Like everything else about this building, there was nothing outwardly special about it, but once he pushed the button to open the door and stepped inside, it was a different story. The elevator was loaded with high-tech security devices out the yin-yang, most of which weren't visible. The Director ignored them since they didn't require him to do anything, and he stepped up to the retinal scanner built into the wall where the floor buttons would be in an ordinary elevator. He leaned his face close to the scanner and waited for it to read his retinal patterns. He never would've admitted this to anyone, especially not his colleagues or subordinates, but he got a kick out of technology, and he always pushed for his agency to have the newest, coolest toys. Sure, it was nominally in the name of national defense, but in reality it was because the Director liked to play with them. Such tech seemed almost like magic, as if there was nothing it couldn't do. But *shouldn't* do? That was a different matter.

Retinal scan complete, the door slid closed and the elevator began to rise.

The Director watched the floor numbers on the digital panel change as the elevator ascended. Aside from the lobby—and where he was headed—every floor of the facility was empty. Though the CIA mainly operated outside the United States, the agency was permitted to deal with issues of foreign intelligence and terrorism on US soil. And if they occasionally overstepped their boundaries… well, you couldn't really fault a fellow for being a patriot now, could you? And if Congress didn't find out, so much the better.

The elevator slowed to a gentle stop and the digital display read COMMAND CENTER. The door slid open, and the Director stepped out into the corridor and began walking with a purposeful stride.

Time for an ass-kicking, he thought.

The instant the elevator door closed, the ceiling panel opened and a dark figure dropped silently into the elevator. He was dressed in black, with short brown hair and beard, intense eyes, and a brow that seemed to be set in a permanent scowl. Hawk straightened and bounced on his feet, eager for action. Hawk waited a few moments to give the Director a chance to move further away from the elevator. He kept bouncing, trying to contain the energy building within him. When he judged that that he'd let enough time pass, he pushed the button to open the elevator door. He stepped out before it was halfway open.

Three men were waiting for the Director as he entered the Command Center's antechamber. They were not just their country's best intelligence operatives; they were among the best spies in the whole goddamn world.

Mr. Pond was a British agent with rugged good looks, and an ever-present smarmy smile who dressed as if he had just come from a formal occasion of some sort—and where he'd probably snuck away with a beautiful counterspy for some hands-on "interrogation." Jonas Borne was CIA, and his detractors thought of him as a muscled pretty boy whose reputation was overblown. Such doubters usually ended up in intensive care—or the morgue. He wore a brown jacket over a black T-shirt—much more casual than Pond's expensive tailored suit—but like Pond, Borne didn't have a hair out of place on his head. Sometimes the Director wondered if the two men exchanged hair-care tips. The third agent was perhaps the deadliest of the three. He wore an old scuffed black leather jacket over a simple black pullover, along with black pants and shoes. Red Erik worked for Russian intelligence, hence his nickname, and unlike the other two spies, his appearance was of no special importance to him. He had a long, narrow face; handsome, but not especially so. He kept his hair buzzed short so he didn't have to deal with it, and he sported several days' growth of stubble. But what truly set him apart from his fellow agents was his eyes. Pond and Borne had no hesitation about killing when the mission demanded it. But Red Erik's eyes glowed with a feral light that marked him as a man who enjoyed killing. And the more he killed, the happier he was.

The Director walked past the trio of spies without acknowledging them. They were the first line of security for this meeting, so despite their much-vaunted reputations, as far as the Director was concerned, tonight they were little more than two-legged watchdogs. He stopped in front of a containment locker, one of several here, opened it, put his three phones—each of which he used for very different but equally covert purposes—inside. Then he closed the door and locked it by touching his thumb to a pigment analyzer pad on the wall.

He continued down the hall to the Command Center's entrance. A handprint reading and another retinal scan, and the door unlocked to admit him. He stepped inside and closed the door behind him. He heard a series of *clicks* and *snicks* as the locks reengaged. A conference table was positioned in the center of the room, on the wall behind it a big-screen TV. On the opposite wall was a large picture window—one-way glass, of course—providing an impressive view of the surrounding buildings. Six spymasters sat at the table, all of whom the Director was acquainted with. Friends, enemies, colleagues, pains in the ass—they were his opposite numbers, heads of intelligence agencies from across the globe. Standing behind them, backs against the walls, were their bodyguards, all of them armed and on high alert. He understood the spymasters' cautiousness—after all, they were far from home—but he considered their desire for protection to be a sign of weakness. To succeed in this game, you needed balls of titanium, and attending a secret meeting with a bodyguard was like admitting you weren't confident, or capable, of defending yourself.

The men sitting at the table were a Who's Who of the world's most ruthless and devious schemers. Aside from the director of the CIA, there were six international spymasters, including the heads of Britain's MI6, the Federal Security Service of the Russian Federation (FSB) and China's Ministry of State Security (MSS). Each one a bastard through and through—at least when the situation demanded it, which in their line of work was more often than not.

On the TV, the President of the United States was giving a speech. "This kind of brazen attack on American soil will not go unpunished. We will be vigilant, and we will find those responsible."

MI6 Control took notice of the Director's entrance and used a remote to mute the volume on the TV. The Director was relieved. He hadn't voted for the sonofabitch, and the man's voice grated on his ears.

All heads turned as his fellow spymasters acknowledged their host's entrance. The Director stopped and regarded them for a moment before speaking.

"Any of you assholes want to make this easy on all of us and just admit you killed Augustus Gibbons?"

MI6 Control frowned. "How do we know it wasn't you?"

"Because I called the goddamn meeting, you Limey prick."

The Director glared around the table at his fellow spymasters, all of who glared right back. The meeting was off to a flying start.

The Director took a seat at the head of the table—naturally—and he gestured for MI6 Control to hand him the remote. The Director pointed it at the TV, pressed a sequence of buttons, and the President was replaced with images of the Dumpling Palace—or rather, the gigantic hole in the ground where the restaurant had once been.

"Dandy of a pipe-blower—that crater must be the size of Wembley Stadium," MI6 Control said.

"It wasn't a bomb." The Director worked the remote and an image of a falling, burning object appeared on the screen, followed by footage of search teams sifting through debris.

"A missile?" the Russian asked.

"No, it wasn't a missile. It was a *satellite*. At terminal velocity, the impact registered over eight kilotons. And without a ballistic heat signature, our long-range detection systems couldn't even see it coming." The Director switched the TV back to the live feed of the President, but he kept it muted.

"You brought us all this way for an accident? Space junk falling from the sky?" the Chinese spymaster said.

"Little paranoid, even for you, George," MI6 Control said.

The Director bristled inwardly at the man's use of his first name. He much preferred being addressed by his title, even by friends, relatives, and lovers. *Especially* lovers.

"Is it paranoia that this particular satellite just happened to be launched less than six days ago by an FSB dummy operation out of Moscow?" the Director countered.

All eyes turned toward the Russian spymaster.

"If Russia wants someone dead, we are behind you with gun and BAM!"

The Director scowled. "That a threat, my friend?"

The Russian scowled back, unintimidated. "Only if you feel threatened, *friend*."

The Director stood up, put his hands palm down on the table, leaned toward the director of the FSB, and unleashed a stream of profanity that would've burned the ears off the most seasoned sailor. Undeterred by the invectives hurled at him, the FSB director followed suit, standing, putting hands on the table, leaning forward, opening his mouth, and giving as good as he was getting. Except, of course, his profanity was in Russian. The other spymasters seated around the table shifted in their seats uncomfortably, and several of the bodyguards put their hands on their sidearms, just in case the situation escalated any further.

Suddenly a piercing whistle cut through the two men's shouting. They quieted at once and turned to see who had made the whistle.

"I brought a tape measure, if that would help you settle things faster."

The woman was a striking blonde in her early forties. She wore a severe white suit jacket and skirt, the lines of the clothing sharp enough to draw blood. She projected an aura of icy confidence, and her eyes shone with fierce, uncompromising intelligence.

This is a dangerous person, the Director thought. Aloud, he said, "Who the hell are you? And how did you get in here?"

"Jane Marke. I'm with the OGA."

"Never heard of you."

"Well then, I guess out of all the swinging dicks in this room, I'm the only one who's any good at her goddamn job."

Marke took a phone from her jacket pocket, entered a number, and waited a moment for the person she was calling to answer.

"Yeah, it's me. Have him give a wave."

She nodded toward the TV, and the Director, along with his fellow spymasters, turned to look at the screen. The President was walking across the Rose Garden after finishing his address. An aide whispered into his ear, and the President stopped, looked to the crowed who'd gathered to listen to him, and waved at them.

"And please burn that tie… Makes him look evasive."

Marke disconnected and replaced the phone in her pocket. Then she turned to the Director and the Russian spymaster. "Okay, you may sit."

The Director exchanged a glance with his FSB counterpart. Neither man spoke a word, but the message that passed between them was clear. *Who the hell does this bitch think she is?* But despite themselves, both men sat.

The Director hadn't been lying when he'd said that he'd never heard of Marke or of the OGA—whatever the hell *that* stood for. And since it was the Director's job to know everything that was worth knowing, this bugged the holy living shit out of him.

Marke reached into another jacket pocket and brought out a handheld device unlike anything the Director had ever seen before. It wasn't just next-gen tech; it was next-*next*-gen.

"Gentlemen," Marke said, "this is the device that crashed the satellite. Nerds in the lab have coined it Pandora's Box."

A figure garbed entirely in black moved across the city's rooftops with the speed and grace of a creature born to this environment. Xiang was a shadow among shadows, a silent silhouette cutting through the night with surgical precision. His mind and body were in perfect balance, fused into a single powerful force directed toward one goal: reaching the anonymous building where some of the world's most dangerous people were holding a secret meeting. By this point, Serena and Hawk were moving into position, and Xiang needed to haul ass if he didn't want to be late for the party.

Despite the intense physical exertion, his breathing was steady, almost relaxed, and his heart rate was surprisingly low. A light sheen of sweat on his forehead was the only outward sign of the effort he was putting forth. His expression was calm, almost placid, as if he were meditating instead of running all out. It was moments like this, nights before an operation kicked into high gear, that he felt most alive, most truly and completely himself. He didn't believe in an afterlife, but he didn't disbelieve, either. There was far too much to contend with in this life for him to concern himself with any other. To Xiang, this was what it meant to truly live.

He poured on the speed as he approached the edge of

a roof and then, without an instant's hesitation, hurled himself out into space.

"My team back-tracked the satellite's last signal input to Miami," Marke said. "Some asshole living it up at the Ritz-Carlton penthouse thought he could hold the world ransom. Three flashbangs, two bullets, and one body bag later, we took custody of the device."

The Director scowled. "You have to be kidding me. There must be at least a hundred redundancies in place to prevent some punk with a laptop hijacking satellites."

"And Pandora's Box can bypass all of them," Marke said. "With a push of a button, it can eavesdrop on secure communications, corrupt military software, transmit false intelligence... or crash a satellite out of the sky like a goddamn tactical warhead."

The Director was no scientist any more than his counterparts were, but when it came to assessing threats, that was their bread and butter. All of them had explored the possibilities of attack by falling satellites before— whether as aggressor, target, or both—and they all had come to the same conclusion: it wouldn't work.

Marke sounded irritated, "Tech like this costs a hell of a lot of money. Only an extremely powerful—and particularly devious—intelligence agency could hope to pull this off, and that means one of you is behind this, and I'm not leaving until I find out who."

That was the moment the Director decided he had put up with more than enough of Marke's shit. He opened his mouth to tell her just that, when the window exploded.

Xiang crashed through the window directly behind Marke. He collided with her, knocking her to the floor, and as he rolled off of her, he snatched Pandora's Box from her hand. Xiang then leaped onto the conference table and held the device out so Marke could see that he'd taken it. Marke had already risen to her feet, and she glared at Xiang with a mixture of surprise and fury. He allowed himself a small smile. Always nice to have one's work appreciated. Marke dove for cover as MI6 Control drew a 9mm and pointed it at Xiang, but before the man could fire, Xiang snatched the weapon from his hand and kicked him in the face, sending the spymaster tumbling backward in his chair. The man's bodyguard reached for his weapon then—a little late on the draw, Xiang thought—and he shot the man through the heart before he managed to raise his gun. As the bodyguard dropped, the man sitting next to MI6— the Mossad spymaster—reached for his own weapon, and Xiang spun around and kicked him in the face, sending him tumbling back to join his fellow spymaster on the floor. Two of the bodyguards that had been standing behind the Mossad director drew their weapons.

Alarms blared then, and steel shutters dropped down over the windows—*Thunk! Thunk! Thunk!* Xiang smiled.

A little late, assholes, he thought. He slipped Pandora's Box into his inner jacket pocket, both to safeguard it and to free up his other hand.

The two guards opened fire then, but Xiang was too fast. He launched himself off the table, glanced in the direction of the Russian spymaster, and then shot one of the attacking bodyguards dead. He shot at the second bodyguard, but missed. Unconcerned with his miss, Xiang turned toward the Russian and gave the man a triple-kick, knocking him down as two more bodyguards began to shoot. Xiang knew all the guards would've started blasting away at him the instant he crashed through the window if they hadn't needed to worry about accidentally shooting their bosses—the very people they had sworn to protect. The guards would continue to be cautious, but the question was for how long?

Xiang jumped back onto the table, landing on his back and spinning around in a maneuver resembling a breakdance move. He fired as he spun, taking out several bodyguards and the Chinese spymaster. As his spin slowed, Xiang's gun clicked empty. He tossed the weapon aside and unzipped his jacket. A bodyguard trained his weapon on Xiang, but before the man could fire, Xiang slipped off his jacket and wrapped it around the bodyguard's arms, trapping the man's weapon inside his jacket. Xiang yanked the jacket toward the ceiling, breaking the bodyguard's grip on the gun. As the weapon flew into the air, Xiang reached up to grab it, then whipped the bodyguard across the face with it. Xiang pulled his jacket free from the man's arms as the man went down, and he tossed it on the table behind him. He caught a flash of motion out of the corner of his eye, and he pointed the gun behind him and fired, taking out another bodyguard who'd been about to shoot him.

Xiang didn't see Marke, and he assumed the woman had taken shelter beneath the table. The CIA director had evidently had enough, for he'd risen from his seat and was heading for the door. Xiang didn't give a damn about the man. His sole objective was to obtain Pandora's Box, so what did he care if the man got away? That meant there would be one less person in the room for him to deal with.

Xiang stood upright on the table and quickly looked around. Two bodyguards on the other side of the table were getting ready to fire at him, and he ran toward them and executed a flying double-kick, striking both men in the face and dropping them to the floor before either could get off a single shot.

His jacket lay on the table in front of him, and as Xiang landed from the kick, he slid toward it, slipped his left arm into the sleeve, turned onto his back, and fired his gun as he continued sliding down the table. A bodyguard armed with an automatic weapon was hit by one of Xiang's bullets, and as he spun around from the impact, his weapon strafed the big-screen TV, causing it to come crashing down as he slumped to the ground, dead. Xiang reached the end of the table, somersaulted backwards— shooting another bodyguard in the process. As he landed, he tossed his gun into the air, finished slipping his jacket all the way on, then caught the gun as it fell.

A bodyguard ran toward him from the other side of the room, but now that Xiang had a few extra seconds to aim, he shot the man in the kneecap instead of going for a killing shot. After all, the man was just doing his job. No need to kill him unless it was necessary. The man howled in pain and dropped his weapon but managed to remain standing. Xiang was impressed. Tough guy.

A glance showed Xiang the CIA director hadn't made it out of the room yet, and now a metal security partition was sliding over the entrance to seal in the attacker— namely Xiang.

Sorry, Tough Guy, Xiang thought. But you're standing between me and freedom.

He stepped onto the man's good leg, up onto his shoulder, and used the man to launch himself toward the room's entrance. The man howled in pain as the force of Xiang's jump put pressure on his injured knee, and this time he fell to the floor, clapping his hands over the wound to staunch the blood loss.

Xiang made it out of the room with only inches to spare. The metal door slammed shut behind him with a loud *thunk!* and a series of locks tripped. The conference room would be on lockdown for at least several minutes, more than long enough for Xiang to escape with his prize. Xiang had landed in a crouching position, and he rose and started walking casually down the hall as if he were out for a leisurely stroll.

Xiang removed Pandora's Box from his jacket pocket and tossed it into the air as he walked. Such a small thing, really, but then small things could sometimes prove to be the most destructive. Look what had happened when humans learned to split the atom.

As Xiang neared the elevator, he saw the American agent—Borne—waiting for him.

"My friends and I heard the shots coming from the conference room. Red Erik thought the bodyguards could handle you, but Pond and I thought they'd fuck it up. Looks like we were right."

Borne's hands curled into fists and he took a step toward Xiang. But Xiang held up a finger, as if to say, *One moment, please.* Borne hesitated, frowning. Xiang checked his watch. *A few more seconds,* he thought.

The elevator door slid open and Hawk came charging out. He slammed into Borne, taking the agent completely by surprise, and the two men crashed through a door on the other side of the hall and into an office. Xiang continued down the hallway, leaving Hawk to go about his work.

* * *

Hawk had heard about Borne. Supposedly he was one of the best agents on the planet, a master at hand-to-hand combat and—when necessary—a deadly killer. So Hawk was prepared to bring his A-game.

As they crashed through the office door, the two men fell onto the floor in a tangle of arms and legs. Borne wriggled away from Hawk, fast and slick as an eel, and got to his feet. He tried to stomp on Hawk's neck, going for a killing strike, but Hawk rolled out of the way and jumped to his feet. Both men were armed, but as if in unspoken agreement, neither drew his weapon. After all, what would be the fun in that?

The office wasn't a large one, and it contained a desk, chair, filing cabinet, and bookshelves. The desk had the usual office equipment sitting on its surface: computer, monitor, office phone, stapler, tape dispenser, a pen and pencil holder—which also contained a metal letter opener—stacks of printouts, scattered paperclips and a couple rubber bands. There was also a coffee mug—half full—on the side of which were the words SPIES DO IT UNDERCOVER.

Hawk took in all these details at a glance, as did Borne, and then they chose their weapons and began combat. Both men went for the letter opener first, naturally, and Borne—who stood marginally closer to the desk than

Hawk—grabbed hold of it first. With a grin, he stepped forward and jabbed the letter opener toward Hawk's throat. Hawk turned to the side to avoid the strike, took hold of the pencil holder, and smashed it against the back of Borne's head. The man doubled over as writing utensils flew through the air and clattered to the floor, along with the holder. Hawk had put all the force behind his strike that he could, but it seemed that Borne's skull was even thicker than he'd thought, for the man recovered quickly and slashed outward with the letter opener. Hawk had to jump back to avoid getting his stomach sliced open, but in doing so, he bumped up against the desk. Borne, seeing Hawk had nowhere to go, moved in for a killing attack, but Hawk grabbed the computer monitor and swung it into Borne's head. The monitor made an extremely satisfying *crunk!* as it connected, and the impact caused the agent to lose his grip on the letter opener. It sailed through the air and became embedded in the wall. Hawk pressed his advantage. He brought the monitor around, intending to strike Borne in the face with it this time, but the agent raised his forearm and blocked the blow. He then yanked the monitor from Hawk's hand and hurled it at him like an awkwardly shaped shuriken. But while the monitor grazed Hawk's right shoulder, it did no real damage. The monitor crashed into the filing cabinet and made a good-sized dent in the metal before bouncing off.

After that, the office became a blur of activity as the

two men grabbed whatever they could reach to use against each other, throwing or hitting. At one point Borne even used a hastily straightened paperclip to try to puncture Hawk's carotid artery.

Now you're just showing off, Hawk thought.

Hawk forced Borne back toward the bookcase. Neither man was seriously injured yet, but Hawk had landed more blows than Borne, and it was clear from the concerned look in the agent's eyes that he wasn't used to anyone being able to put up a real fight against him. He was slowing down and starting to look more than a little desperate. He glanced behind him at the bookshelf and pulled off the thickest hardback he could find.

Before Borne could attack again, Hawk snatched the book from his hands.

"You fight me with a book?" Moving faster than Borne could react, Hawk smacked the large book against his face repeatedly. *Thwack-thwack-thwack-thwack-thwack!* "Here you go, brother. Page one, chapter one."

Borne staggered, eyes unfocused. Hawk followed the series of strikes with a final devastating blow to the side of Borne's head. The man's eyes rolled white and he collapsed to the floor, unconscious.

Hawk tossed the book down on Borne's chest.

"Shit happens."

Hawk walked out of the office and hurried to catch up to Xiang.

* * *

Xiang and Hawk raced down the stairs three at a time. Pandora's Box was once more safely tucked away in Xiang's jacket pocket, and he gave a grim smile. *So far, everything is going—*

The two men stopped as they saw the exit was blocked by a steel security door that had no doubt dropped into place the second alarms started blaring. Neither Xiang nor Hawk seemed especially concerned about finding their only escape route blocked. Xiang stepped up to the door and rapped a knuckle against the surface, tapping out the old "Shave and a Haircut" rhythm. A moment later, sparks flew from the door as someone began cutting through the metal with an acetylene torch.

—according to plan, Xiang thought.

Serena cut the last lock on the security door, and she turned off the torch as Xiang and Hawk shoved the door open and joined her on the other side. She smiled a greeting, but then she frowned as she thought she detected a soft scuffling sound coming from around the corner. It sounded like a shoe sliding across the floor— done deliberately to lure an opponent? Maybe, Serena thought. She smiled. And if that was the case, she'd hate to disappoint the scuffer. She motioned for Xiang and Hawk to remain where they were, then she lay the torch down next to the acetylene tank. She then walked down the hall and turned the corner to see what surprise might await her.

Mr. Pond stood leaning against the wall, arms crossed casually over his chest.

"Sorry, darling," he said in his oh-so-proper British accent. "Private party."

He uncrossed his arms, reached for his watch, and touched a control on the side. *Zztt* sounds emerged from the device, along with a pair of tiny projectiles. Pond gave a half-smile as the micro-darts—which Serena assumed were coated with one deadly poison or another—streaked toward her. She stood there, unconcerned, and just as the darts were about to strike, her hands blurred and she plucked them out of the air as easily as pulling petals off a flower.

Pond gaped at her, stunned, and as she tossed the darts aside and started walking calmly toward Pond, the British agent yanked off his bowtie and hurled it at her. The cloth was lined with razor wire and was weighted at both ends, making it a combination of a bolo and a garrote. Serena dodged this new device easily, and the wire *whiffed* past her without doing any harm.

Pond looked more than a little worried now. He reached into his inner jacket pocket, pulled out a fountain pen, and pointed it at Serena. He depressed a button and it disgorged a cloud of noxious-smelling green gas.

Serena simply held her breath and walked through the cloud, unaffected.

When she reached Pond, she grabbed his balls in an iron grip and slammed him back against the wall.

"Invitation must've got lost in the mail," she said, and then added, "*Darling.*"

She leaned her face toward his and licked her lips before parting them slightly. Pond's eyes widened in surprise at first, but then renewed confidence came over him. Now he was back on familiar ground.

But instead of kissing the man, Serena headbutted him. The agent's eyes rolled up in his head, and he slid to the floor, out cold.

A moment later, Xiang and Hawk joined her, and without more than a disdainful glance at the British agent, the three of them continued down the hallway.

They made it to ground level without encountering any other obstacles, and a moment later they were out on the street. An Asian man with platinum-blond dyed hair wearing a long-sleeved black pullover came running up to them, breathing hard and trying to catch his breath.

"You're late," Xiang said, not bothering to consult his watch. He wasn't surprised, though. Talon was almost always late, and that meant Xiang was almost always irritated with him.

Before Talon could reply, a loud engine *vroomed*, and

they all turned to see Red Erik waiting for them on top of a Ducati SuperSport motorcycle. The Russian was parked across the street, facing them.

"Naw, I'm just in time, boss."

Red Erik revved the engine again, the deep thrum echoing up and down the street.

"Nobody gets past me."

Red Erik peeled out and came racing toward them. Talon started running toward the bike in what looked like the most one-sided game of chicken the world would ever see. Erik popped a wheelie, but Talon didn't hesitate. He kept on running. Erik drew a pistol and started firing. But Talon performed a series of rapid handsprings, flipping end over end, too fast for the bullets to find him. When he was close to Erik, he launched himself into the air, landing a mighty kick to Erik's neck and knocking the man off his bike. Erik lay on the asphalt, unconscious, as Talon hopped onto the bike's seat and took control, popping a front wheelie of his own before stopping in front of Xiang, Serena, and Hawk.

Xiang knelt next to the semi-conscious superspy and gazed down at the man.

"We ain't nobody," he said.

Inside the conference room, the Director and MI6 Control watched as the dead were zipped into body bags and hauled away. Both men had been at this game so long they'd thought nothing could surprise them anymore. Tonight, they'd found out differently.

Marke—who like the two men had managed to survive the attack unscathed—walked over to join them.

"And though the gods begged Pandora to never open the box, she was vain and naïve, and she loosed upon the world every evil to which humanity is heir," Marke said.

"So how do we get it back?" the British spymaster asked.

"These assholes just took out the best of the best like it was Sunday brunch. We need someone who can move like them, fight like them. We need someone who can walk into a tornado and come out the other side like it was a damn gentle breeze."

"And you know someone like that?" the Director asked.

"No," Marke said. "But Gibbons did."

2

THE DOMINICAN REPUBLIC

Xander Cage clung to a massive antennae array. He was free-climbing—no rope, no net, no second chances. Just the way he liked it. He wore a gray sleeveless shirt, white pants, brown boots, along with a backpack and black gloves with metal covering the fingertips and knuckles. He paused to look behind him and gazed upon a verdant valley below, no sign of civilization as far as the eye could see. Right then, he felt like the king of the fucking world. He could hang here all day, admiring the view and breathing the fresh air, but he had work to do, and he'd best get to it.

He resumed climbing and when he reached the top, he pulled out his phone to check the clock. He'd set the timer to run a countdown before starting his climb, and the display told him he had exactly ten minutes left. Better hurry. He drew a knife from a sheath on his belt and quickly cut through a tangle of wires. He then pulled an object free and stuffed it in his backpack.

"You there! Stop!"

Xander looked down to see several uniformed and very angry-looking security guards standing at the base of the array. He wasn't going to be able to leave that way, but it was no big deal. He'd planned on a much more fun descent. He sheathed his knife and then reached into his backpack, removed a pair of half-skis, and quickly attached them to his boots while the security guards continued to yell up at him. Then, without so much as a split-second of hesitation, Xander leaped off the array, soaring over the security guards as he fell.

He crashed into the canopy and plummeted between a pair of trees, using his metal-gloved hands to slow his fall. He hit the sloping ground and began dry-surfing through the foliage, in and out, over and under, a quick-draw slalom through gates only he could see, going for the gold. Carving dirt, jumping rocks, grinding fallen trees, leaves and branches slapping him as he raced past, birds and small animals getting the hell out of his way as fast as they could. At one point there was a gap in the green, and when he glanced to the side, he saw a large flock of bats keeping pace with him. He came to a patch of ground that had a small ridge to it, and he used it to launch himself into the air, eyes closed. Everything around him was still, wind in his face, sun on his back. For an instant, he felt as if time had been suspended, and he could remain like this forever, *feel* like this forever. It was the closest to religion that he ever came, this sensation of being connected to something far larger than himself—wild, strong, primal. He was more fully himself in micro-moments like these— more *complete*—than at any other time.

Xander shot off an overhang, dropped through the air a dozen feet and landed on the roof of an old shack, sending up a cloud of dust. He kicked off his half-skis, slid over the edge of the roof, and dropped to the ground. A gang of local kids were waiting for him there, and one boy came forward. He held a homemade longboard with xXx painted on it, and he handed it to Xander with a grin. Xander grinned back, put the board on the ground, stepped on, and began skating down a narrow mountain road, accompanied by the sound of the kids cheering him on. As he raced down the long, twisting road, he checked the time on his phone once more. This was going to be close…

Xander didn't need a speedometer to know how fast he was going. He knew speed the same way other people knew their own reflection.

45 mph.

55 mph.

65 mph.

Faster, faster, faster.

He took turns without slowing down, crouching low,

leaning through the hairpins, hands working as rudders, his metal gloves sending up sparks from the pavement.

He came to an area with several small shops, and the locals chased after him yelling and cheering.

"Ex, Ex, Ex!"

The road leveled off here, and he began to slow down. He latched into the driver's side door of a passing car. The window was down, and the driver—an old man—looked at him, startled.

"*Mi Pana, dame un chance.*" <Hey, Bro, give me a chance.>

The man broke out in a broad grin and gave Xander a high five, then he whipped his car around a corner, pulling Xander with him.

The instant they rounded the corner, Xander saw the road sloped downhill once more, and the car picked up speed, Xander along with it. Xander was about to thank his benefactor, release his grip on the car, and continue on down alone, when he saw a massive dump truck chugging up the hill toward them, the vehicle so large it took up the entire road, which hadn't been all that wide to begin with. Xander didn't panic, though. Instead, a deep calm settled on him, a zen-like meditative state. He hadn't felt this relaxed, this *centered*, in months.

I gotta record this, he thought.

The driver of the car pressed down on his brake, giving Xander an apologetic look. Xander told him it was no problem, thanked him for the assist, and pushed away from the vehicle. He rolled downhill toward the dump truck, picking up speed quickly. The driver of the truck laid on his horn as a warning—as if Xander could possibly have missed seeing the huge fucking thing. He crouched down on his board, reached into his backpack, pulled out his GoPro and hit RECORD. He held the device selfie-style as he rocketed toward the truck.

Just as he was about to hit the vehicle head-on, Xander swerved and—after catching a glimpse of the driver's terrified face—he zipped around the passenger side of the truck, the wheels of his board less than a half-inch from the road's edge, his body even closer to the vehicle. Then he was past and racing downhill unimpeded once more.

Thread that needle, baby! he thought.

Now that he'd gotten his shot, he turned off his GoPro, tucked it into his backpack once more, and continued racing down the road.

A short time later Xander held onto the bumper of a truck filled with goats and children. When the truck drew near the Salt Mine Camp, he let go. He shot toward a car and leaped off his board. He sailed over the vehicle while his board slipped underneath, but he didn't attempt to land on it. The ground in the camp was too level and rocky for boarding, and since he had almost no time left, he would have to go the rest of the way on foot. He hit the ground running, and he heard his board flip over and skid across rock. He'd probably have to touch up the paint job when this was all over. He tore off his gloves, tossed them aside, and checked his timer. 00:30. 00:29. 00:28…

He slipped off his backpack and held it in one hand as he ran for all he was worth toward the ocean, flashing past mine workers and their families, heading for a small hut on the pier. Thirty pissed-off miners were crowded into the hut, waiting, most of them armed and all of them glowering at him. Xander ran to the bar, pulled the small satellite dish he'd "borrowed" from the array out of his pack, set it on the counter, and connected it to a wall jack as the miners watched, grumbling and whispering.

00:03, 00:02, 00:01…

A big-screen TV at the back of the bar switched on just in time for the World Cup Final kick-off. The bar erupted in cheers, whistles, and applause, and then everyone turned their attention to the game as it began.

Xander stood off to the side, watching the happy miners with a feeling of deep satisfaction. Kunal—the boy who'd had Xander's longboard ready for him at the shack—came up to him. Kunal said he'd put Xander's gloves and longboard in his hut, and Xander thanked him.

"*Sabio que lo harias, Xander. Nos entregaste el mundo.*" <I knew you would do it, Xander. You brought the world to us.>

"*El mundo es grande pero siempre cabe en to corazón.*

Llevalo contigo siempre. Go, go!" <The world is big but always fits in your heart. Take it with you always. Go, join them! Go!>

Kunal ran to watch the game along with the others.

"Why not pay the satellite company to watch the game like a regular guy?"

Xander turned to Lola. He'd heard her come up behind him—he always did—but he'd waited for her to speak before acknowledging her presence. She said it creeped her out whenever he turned around just before she started to speak, like he was a wolf who'd caught her scent long before she arrived. He didn't tell her that he *could* smell her.

Lola wasn't simply beautiful. She was *gorgeous*, the kind of woman who seemed almost unearthly, as if she were a work of fine art come to life, an idealized image that had stepped out of a painting or a statue transformed into flawless flesh. She was nearly six feet tall, with long auburn hair and brown eyes, and she wore a white sleeveless top with white shorts. As always when Xander saw her, his breath caught in his throat, and it took a second before he could speak.

"What for? To line the pocket of some boardroom billionaires? Baby, these days regular guys just can't afford to be regular anymore."

"You know, none of them believed you were ever coming back," Lola said.

"And what did you believe?"

"I'm happy."

"Happier than they are?" He gestured to the miners gathered around the TV in the bar.

She stepped forward and put a hand on his chest. "I really missed you."

"I never made a promise I couldn't keep."

She smiled then, a little sadly.

"I don't know about that," she said.

They walked away from the bar, the setting sun behind them, cheers from the crowd in the bar floating on the air.

They rode a salt car down the long track that ran through the camp, the driver studiously looking the other way as Lola straddled Xander, kissing his neck and face. When the car drew near Xander's hut, the driver stopped and they got out.

"*Grazias*," Xander said, and gave the man a few coins as a tip.

They smiled and held hands as they walked, children playing all around them. The moment they were inside the hut, they turned to each other and kissed. It was their first passionate kiss of the evening, but it was far from their last.

Several hours later, Xander and Lola—tired, a bit sore, but relaxed and contented—lay atop the hut's roof, gazing up at the night sky. After a time, Lola began speaking.

"My grandfather used to say the stars were put in the sky as a map for lost travelers. Now he says there are too many stars. The sky is wrong; the gods have gone crazy. How will anyone find their way home now? The lost will never return."

"Your *abuelo* would've been right—one hundred years ago," Xander said. "Unfortunately, these days no one stays lost forever. Every debt gets settled."

"Even out here on the edge of the universe?"

"Yeah, even out here."

"Everybody needs a place in the world," she said.

"No, that's a lie they want us to believe. It sounds good, but does the world really provide a place for people? The game's rigged, and the house always wins. And if you somehow manage to get ahead in life, you know what they do?"

"What?"

"They go and change the rules on you. The world needs me? I say bullshit. I don't owe the world anything."

"True," Lola said. "I just feel like you're gonna leave me."

Xander glanced upward then, as if responding to some preternatural instinct. He saw a shooting star flash across the sky and then vanish. Except he didn't think it was a meteorite. It was something more mundane—and far more troubling.

"Would it make tomorrow easier if you knew tonight?" he asked.

"You always say that. Stay lost with me. I know you are happy here. I mean, look at it. We're in paradise!"

"And if I stay, I'm gonna jeopardize this paradise. That wasn't a shooting star, baby."

"What are you talking about?"

"That was what they call an M-9 Air Force Reaper Drone, about a thousand miles from its base."

"What was it doing? Looking for you?"

Xander nodded. "Coming to settle a debt."

They were both silent for a moment, and when Lola spoke again, her tone was deliberately light, as if she wanted to avoid the subject of the drone—and what it might mean for the two of them.

"You still haven't taught me how to ride that longboard of yours."

"Oh, is that all you like me for? Only one rule."

"What's that?"

Instead of answering, he leaned over and kissed her.

Later that night, Xander lay in bed next to Lola, staring up at the ceiling. From the soft, steady rhythm of her breathing, he knew she was sleeping. He was glad one of them was getting some rest. A fire was burning outside, probably warming some miners sleeping off the effects of their post-soccer celebration. Flickering orange light came in through the window, creating dancing shadows on the hut's walls and ceiling. As he lay there, knowing that he was going to have to leave at dawn, he found himself thinking back to more than a decade ago, when he'd decided to fake his own death and go off the grid—*all* the way off.

He rolled over and put an arm across Lola. She didn't wake, but she smiled in her sleep and snuggled closer to him. Xander closed his eyes, but he didn't sleep. He didn't want to. He wanted to listen to Lola breathe for as long as he could, for he knew that after tonight, he would never hear it again.

Lola woke in the morning to find Xander gone. She wasn't surprised, not after what he had said last night. But what *did* surprise her was that he'd left his longboard— the paint retouched where it had gotten scraped off yesterday—next to her on the bed. There was a post-it note on the board containing a short message written in Xander's handwriting: RULE #1: DON'T FALL.

She smiled.

Xander sat on a bench at an open-air bus station in a town plaza several miles away from the Salt Mine Camp. He was looking at a world map covered in red X's. The X's represented all the places he'd been in his life, all places he could never return to—not unless he wanted whoever was looking for him to find him, that is. He'd moved around frequently over the last ten years in order to remain dead to the world, and the hardest part—after leaving behind the few people he allowed himself to grow close to in each place, of course—was finding somewhere new to go. There weren't too many places he hadn't been, and it had gotten to the point where he might have to give some serious thought to moving to Antarctica. They had penguins down there, so that was a plus. Penguins were cool.

An old man sat down on the bench next to Xander. He carried a duffle bag which he tucked beneath the bench. He then sat up, glanced over at Xander, and then down at his map.

"World getting smaller?" the man said. He smiled. "I know the feeling."

Xander turned to the old man and stared at him, unspeaking.

The man went on, seemingly unbothered by Xander's lack of response. "Running from your problems never works out, you know. You need a new plan."

"Gramps, I think I just need a new map."

"Well, don't say I didn't warn you." The man smiled again, but this time there was an edge to it that Xander didn't like.

"Yeah," Xander said, "like I *need* a warning."

The old man got up and walked away. Xander watched the man go, thinking that the encounter hadn't just been weird—it had been straight-up *suspicious*. He immediately scanned the crowd in the plaza. A teenager sat on the floor air-drumming while music blared from his Beats by Dre headphones. A woman hurried past, obviously late for her bus. A security guard was buying a bottle of soda from a station vendor. Everything *seemed* okay, but that was the problem. It was a little *too* okay, and Xander started to think that it might be a good idea to get the hell out of here before—

That's when he realized the old man had left his duffle bag. *Don't do it,* he told himself. But Xander bent down, took the duffle from under the bench, and sat it next to him. He unzipped it slowly, and when nothing happened, he pulled it open to find enough explosives to level the bus station and probably most of the plaza, too.

"Oh boy. Here we go again."

As if that was a cue, a SWAT team came charging onto the platform, weapons hot.

"Don't move, asshole!" the SWAT captain shouted.

Civilians scattered in all directions as a dozen armed men and women surrounded Xander and trained their weapons on him. Xander, for his part, stood up and watched the officers calmly.

The captain stepped forward, raised his assault rifle, and aimed it at a point directly between Xander's eyes. "On your knees, you son of a bitch!" he shouted, spittle flying from his lips.

"Okay," Xander said, "I'm trying to comply, but you're

confusing me. Which is it? 'Don't move, asshole' or 'On your knees, you son of a bitch?'"

The SWAT team moved in closer, grips tightening on their weapons, eyes gleaming as if they were already picturing Xander's bullet-riddled body lying on the ground.

Xander smiled. "Dude, you're *horrible* at this."

"Three seconds to comply!" the captain shouted, moving even closer to Xander. "One!"

"I'm just trying to help you," Xander said.

"Two!"

"Three," Xander finished for him.

He reached out and snatched the assault rifle from the captain's hands. He kicked the man in the chest, sending him flying backward, and then he fired point blank on the SWAT team. He fired until the clip was empty and then lowered the weapon. Xander was not surprised to see the men and women still standing there, uninjured. The rifle had been loaded with blanks, just as he'd known it would be.

"Okay, come out, come out, wherever you are," he called in a sing-song voice.

A blond woman in a white suit—who had taken cover behind the bench she had been seated on when the SWAT team appeared—now stood and came walking toward Xander.

"Olly-olly-oxen-free," the woman said.

The civilians who had fled came out of hiding now, and the SWAT officers—including the one Xander had knocked down—moved back to give Xander and the woman room to talk.

"Wow, you *do* look different, Gibbons," Xander said. "What is it? The hair? Did you lose weight?"

Despite his flippant words, Xander was assessing the woman as she approached him. She was clearly in charge here, and pretty high up on the pecking order too from the way everyone instantly deferred to her. She exuded the confidence of someone who was used to getting what she wanted without having to ask, and who expected her orders to be carried out before she'd finished giving them. To put it simply, she was the Boss.

"Augustus always had such… well, not exactly *nice* things to say about you, but his eulogy at your funeral was quite affecting. When did you realize this was all a fake?"

"From the start," Xander said. "I've seen better acting in a reality show. I mean, you got a kid over there wearing $800 headphones when you can buy the five-dollar knockoff right down the street. That lady running for the bus that doesn't leave for another two hours, and the security guard paying for a soda with American money. But the kicker was when Clarence from *It's a Wonderful Life* sits next to a tatted-up beast like me with a bag of bombs, and he just happens to know that I speak English. Come on."

"The bullets could have been real," the woman pointed out.

"Then their body armor woulda been, too. Here, I believe this belongs to you."

Xander handed the assault rifle to the woman and continued speaking.

"Look, I don't know who you are, but I don't like being tested."

"Gibbons never believed you were dead. He never stopped looking for you. Hell of a friend."

"Yeah? Well, the joke's on him. We were never friends."

"Trust me, he's not laughing. Nor will he ever again, for that matter."

The woman's words hit Xander like a sledgehammer blow to the gut.

"What did you say your name was?" he asked.

The woman—who introduced herself as Marke—escorted him to an old church off the plaza. As they walked, she gave him a quick rundown of why she'd sought him out—and what had happened to Gibbons. The church was empty, naturally, and she led him to a pew where a computer tablet rested. She picked up the tablet, swiped her finger across the screen to activate it, and then handed it to Xander. A series of images appeared, three men and a woman, their faces mostly obscured by shadows and bad angles. Still frames from security camera footage, Xander guessed.

"Three of the world's best killers stepped into the ring with these four, and not one could so much as draw blood. I was hoping you'd be interested in headlining the next fight card."

It was hard to tell from the poor-quality images, but if they really had gone up against the biggest and baddest the world's intelligence agencies had to offer without so much as getting scratched, they weren't just good: they were *damn* good.

"And locate the Pandora's Box that you lost," he said.

"Well, everybody's in it for something," Marke said. "I'm just upfront about it."

"At least you admit it." The image on the tablet changed to an outer view of a building in what Xander guessed was Manhattan. He zoomed in on the image to get a better look and saw the shattered remains of a picture window. It wasn't difficult to figure out what had happened. "Whoa. Seventy feet across, ninety feet down, three-inch-thick security glass."

Marke nodded. "No rope, no line, no chute."

"C'mon, that's *impressive*. They must've had a blast!"

Marke ignored the comment. "We've run facial IDs on every database in the world, and we couldn't even match a speeding ticket for any of them. They're ghosts in a day and age where that sort of thing is all but impossible."

Xander handed the tablet back to her. "You can

probably guess that I don't work for suits, so why would I spoil their fun?"

"If you won't do it for me, do it for Gibbons."

Xander knew better than to fall for such obvious emotional manipulation. He started walking back down the aisle to the church entrance.

Marke called out after him. "Your country needs you, Mr. Cage. No more hiding. Time to be a patriot."

Xander kept walking as he answered. "I wasn't hiding. I was taking a long vacation. And patriot? By whose definition? I was once down three strikes, and there was only one man who believed in an underdog. *He* was a patriot. No such thing as patriotism anymore, though. Only rebels and tyrants."

"So which are you?" Marke asked.

Xander stopped. He thought about the boy lying in the street, half his head gone, dead before he'd even learned to drive. The tyrants of the world ground people like that boy underneath their heels just for shits and giggles. Maybe the world needed more rebels, if for no other reason than so people like that boy would have somebody to fight for them when they couldn't fight for themselves.

He turned around to face Marke.

"I'm Xander fucking Cage."

Marke smiled. "Welcome back, Triple-X."

He looked at her for a long moment before turning

once more and continuing toward the church entrance.

"Where are you going?" Marke said, sounding concerned, as if she was worried he was going to leave her high and dry after all.

"London," he said.

"Why? What's in London?"

"A ghost hunter."

He walked out of the church and kept on going.

3

Xander stood on a roof in the center of the city. The night air was a bit chilly, and there was a breeze, but he was more than warm enough in his trademark fur coat. It felt good to be wearing it again, almost like coming home.

Don't start getting sentimental, he told himself. *It's just a coat.* But then again, he did look damn good in it.

A pair of stunningly beautiful women armed with assault rifles and wearing black bikinis stood at the edge of a heated pool built into the roof. They looked like something out of an NRA member's wet dream, but if either of them felt the cold, they didn't show it. They appeared completely comfortable and relaxed, but Xander knew they were keeping a close eye on him, and if he did anything they didn't liked, they'd shoot his dick off before he could blink. He wasn't worried, though. He'd only come

67

here to speak with an old friend—and ask for her help.

He smiled at the women. "I'm reminded of freediving the lakes off Prague."

Neither of them responded, and their expressions didn't change. For all the response they'd shown, they might not have heard him. *Can't blame a guy for trying,* he thought.

The friend he'd come to visit was beneath the water, swimming through the blue with silent ease, as if she'd been born to it. After a couple moments, she broke the surface and climbed the steps out of the pool. She wore a black two-piece swimsuit that showed off her lithe body—along with the ankle monitor attached to one leg. Although she was no longer in the water, she still moved with the same elegant grace as she had in the pool. One of the armed women was waiting for her, and she held out a white cashmere robe.

Before the woman could take the robe, Xander said, "Allow me."

The guard gave her employer a questioning look, and after a moment's thought, she nodded, and the guard passed the robe to Xander. He stepped forward, slipped it on the woman, and walked around to embrace her. She hugged him back, but she pulled away from him after only a couple seconds.

"Hello, Ainsley," he said. Her long blond hair was wet and hugged the contours of her shoulders and back. She had full lips that, as far as Xander knew, were naturally tinted red, and she possessed elegant, almost regal features. Her eyes were a dark cool blue—*Atlantic Ocean blue,* Xander thought—and they hinted at unknown depths within. A classical old-world beauty, she looked like she'd descended from a long line of noble blood, and who knows? Perhaps she had.

"X." Her tone was cool and reserved, but Xander detected the undertone of affection in it.

He turned and looked out over the city. "I forgot how good the view is up here."

"This kind of real estate is out of your price range, believe me. I see you've found your coat."

"You said you'd take good care of it."

"I did."

Ainsley started toward a poolside cabana where two other women—also beautiful and also in bikinis—sat on a chaise lounge working behind glowing laptops. Xander followed. He removed an iPad from his coat and passed it to one of the women, who took it without looking at him and placed it on the seat beside her. On the screen were images from the New York break-in.

"I'm looking for someone," he said.

"Since when have we ever had a business relationship?" Ainsley asked, sounding a bit irritated. "I get caught even *touching* a computer, my ass goes away for twenty."

Ainsley King was one of the best hackers the world

had ever seen, a virtuoso on a keyboard, a genius who understood software as if she had been born with a high-speed computer in place of a brain. Xander wouldn't have been surprised if she had fiber-optic cable running through her body in place of a circulatory system. She used her skills in the employ of governments, corporations, and obscenely wealthy individuals. Her rates were sky-high, but she was worth it, and because of this she had become obscenely wealthy herself. Unfortunately, she fell into a trap set by Interpol. To avoid a lengthy prison stay, she accepted house arrest and twenty-four-hour monitoring, and agreed to provide data on some of her more... *questionable* clients to Interpol. As far as Xander knew, she hadn't gone near a computer since, but she was the only one who could help him track down the thieves who'd stolen Pandora's Box, and he needed her help. He quickly gave her a rundown of what had happened in New York.

When he was finished, he said, "Come on. Name your price. You know I'm good for it."

"Oh, X, that's adorable. Information like this doesn't have a price."

If money wasn't going to motivate her, Xander thought, maybe appealing to her professional pride would. "If you don't think you can find them—if you've lost your edge— just tell me. I'll understand."

She scowled at that, and Xander knew his jab had hit home.

"You want to know what it really is, Cage? I used to think you were The Man, but now maybe I'm worried that you're just working for him."

Ainsley's counterpunch landed a solid hit. Xander wasn't comfortable working with Marke, and he sure as hell didn't trust the woman, not like he'd trusted Gibbons. He decided to play it off as a joke though. "Ouch. Now that's hitting below the belt. Come on, no one knows I'm here, and you know how excellent I am at keeping a secret."

He stepped a little closer to her and was gratified when she didn't back away.

"So you say. But Interpol's got these new listening bugs. Practically invisible, real MI5 kinda shit. Disappear under your skin, under your arms, tied around your balls like a Christmas bow."

Xander grinned wide and took another step closer. Now there was less than an inch of space separating them. "So unwrap me then."

Ainsley looked into his eyes, her expression unreadable. "Do you know that studies have proven sexual consummation irrevocably ruins nine out of ten relationships?"

"Lucky for me you love to gamble."

"Of course…"

She leaned in to him, so close that her lips almost brushed his, but at the last instant she pulled back.

"…not," she finished. "My friends, on the other hand, adore stiff odds."

"Stiff odds? What does that—"

The two women in the cabana closed their laptops and slid them underneath the chaise. As they came toward Xander the two guards—their weapons stowed somewhere—entered the cabana. Without another word Ainsley picked up the tablet Xander had brought, pushed past him, and headed back for the pool while her four assistants began to "strip search" him. Xander smiled.

"Christmas comes earlier every year."

The next morning Xander was putting on a black muscle shirt when one of his four companions stirred. Since the women—all naked—slept close together on the chaise, the movement of one disturbed the others. Xander thought they might wake, but they settled back down, and soon the quartet was sleeping deeply once more. Considering the workout they'd all had last night, he wouldn't mind getting some more Z's, but he wanted to see what Ainsley had turned up while her staff had kept him entertained—and vice versa. He finished dressing, gave the women a last look, and smiled.

"The things I do for my country—but I ain't complaining. Take the rest of the day off, ladies."

He left the cabana and went in search of Ainsley.

* * *

Ainsley had left a message for Xander to meet her at a coffee shop down the street called Balzac's. Evidently her "house arrest" extended a bit further than most people's. Either that was part of her deal with Interpol, or she'd tinkered with the monitoring device to increase its range.

Xander entered the shop and saw Ainsley sitting at a table near a window. He nodded to her then went to the counter to order.

"Excuse me," he said, putting on a British accent, "can I have a cup of coffee? Black."

"Sure," the barista said. The woman poured his coffee and handed it to him.

"What do I owe you for that? Five quid?" Xander handed her the money. "Keep the change." He then joined Ainsley at the table, took off his coat, draped it over a chair, and sat down.

She shook her head. "Are you still taking the piss out of me with that accent? All these years, and you're all over the place. Manchester meets Liverpool meets Newcastle meets who the hell knows where? Essex?"

Ainsley wore a sleeveless white top and black running pants with white stripes. Xander preferred the way she looked in a bikini, but he knew better than to mention it.

"As long as I don't sound like I'm from Jersey," he said.

"Oh, okay." Ainsley said in a dead-on Jersey accent. "Yep."

She took a sip of her tea and pushed a napkin across

the table toward him. He saw there was an envelope hidden underneath.

"Like finding needles in a stack of needles," she said. Her eyes were slightly red, and Xander knew she'd been up most of the night working on getting him the information he needed. She might be tired, but the pride she took in her success was clear in her voice.

"Even if you are shackled by the Queen, you're the best in the world." He reached for the napkin, but Ainsley pulled it back before he could take it.

"You know why no one else could find them?" she asked.

"Why?"

"*They don't exist*—and they want to keep it that way. Do yourself a favor: take the envelope and burn it. The whispers I hear… These ghosts of yours are the real kind of trouble. They have training, funding, and absolutely no problem running over anyone who gets in their way."

He smiled. "You worried about me getting hurt?"

"I'm worried about you getting dead," she said bluntly.

"I'm really touched that you could picture the world without me in it, Ainsley."

She shrugged. "It would be a little less fun is all I'm saying."

"Thank you." He reached over and took the napkin with the envelope it covered.

Ainsley took another sip of her tea. "At least we'll

finally answer the age-old question."

"Which is what?"

"Who wins in a fight: immovable object or unstoppable force?"

Xander grinned. "Sister, if you don't already know the answer, then you haven't been paying attention."

It had started raining while Xander was in the coffee shop with Ainsley, and now he walked down the sidewalk through pouring rain. A couple blocks from Balzac's, an SUV pulled over the curb next to him. He climbed in the back seat where Marke was waiting for him and closed the door. The driver immediately pulled back into traffic and moved off. Xander handed her the piece of paper Ainsley had given him, and her eyes widened as she read it.

"Your ghosts are hanging in the Philippines," he said. "Figures they'd go to the South Pacific, have a little jungle rave off the grid."

Marke looked up from the paper and frowned at him. "How the hell did you find them so quickly?"

Xander smiled. "Undercover work."

THE PHILIPPINES

Serena walked across an unnamed beach on an unnamed island. She wore a black sundress and sandals. The sky was the bluest of any she'd ever seen, and the clouds were so white they almost seemed to shine with their own internal light source. The water was a vivid blue-green, and the sand looked like powdered sugar. The temperature was in the mid-eighties, but with the breeze coming off the sea, it felt ten degrees cooler. It would've been the most beautiful place she had ever been, she thought, if it hadn't been for the people. The beach was filled with gun runners and drug smugglers, all looking to enjoy themselves while laying low and hiding from whoever might be searching for them. Bricks of pot stoked campfires while island girls ran drinks down from a dilapidated temple up on a nearby hillside. The air was filled with shouting, cursing, laughing, and singing, but Serena ignored the chaos as she walked toward the pier. She wasn't in any mood to be around a bunch of drunk and stoned assholes right now. She was royally pissed, and she wanted answers—*now*.

Xiang, wearing a white T-shirt and jeans, stood at the end of the pier, smoking a cigarette and looking out toward the horizon in quiet contemplation, as was his custom. Serena charged down the pier toward him, and while she was certain he heard her, he didn't turn around as she approached. On the pier near his feet sat several coconuts, plastic straws sticking out of holes that had been chopped into their tops with machetes. People loved to open a fresh coconut and pour in rum to mix with the milk inside. It made for a tasty drink.

"Where is it?" she demanded.

Xiang didn't bother asking what *it* was or pretending he didn't know what she was talking about. "In a safe place."

Serena's hands balled into fists, and it took every bit of control she had not to take a swing at Xiang. "That wasn't part of the plan."

"After all these years together, you're still shocked when I improvise?"

"No, but the mission was to destroy it."

Now Xiang turned to face her. He paused to take a drag on his cigarette and answered as he exhaled smoke. "Turns out there's a new mission."

"Really? The whole world is looking for us, Xiang."

"Let them come. The greatest warrior the world has ever known was killed with a pebble. Imagine what we can do with a rock. You're worried about the pawn sacrifice, but I got my eye on the King."

He turned back toward the ocean, as if he considered the matter settled. Serena was far from finished, though. Pandora's Box wasn't merely a piece of super-sophisticated tech. It was *evil*, and no good could ever come of it, regardless of who used it or their motivation for doing so. She'd worked with Xiang for a long time now, and she not only trusted him, she respected him. But he could get tunnel vision when he was focused on a goal—especially if it was a cause he believed in. That focus made him one of the best at what he did, but it sometimes blinded him to the potential consequences of his choices. And once he had his mind set on a course of action, it was almost impossible to convince him to alter his plan.

She looked at Xiang's back, and with only an instant's hesitation, she drew her Glock.

"That's the problem—you forgot about the Queen."

She fired three rounds in rapid succession. But instead of putting bullets into Xiang, she blasted the discarded coconuts near his feet. They exploded into pieces, some of which landed on the pier, some of which flew into the water, and some of which struck Xiang's legs. He hadn't flinched as she fired, and now he took another drag on his cigarette, seemingly unconcerned.

Having made her point, Serena holstered her Glock, turned, and walked away.

This isn't over, she thought. *Not by a long shot.*

RAF WELFORD, BERKSHIRE

Marke led Xander through a crowded terminal where NSA agents worked double-time to pack gear and equipment. Royal Air Force Welford was located approximately fifty miles west-southwest of London. During World War II, both the Royal Air Force and the United States Army Air Forces used the base primarily as a transport airfield. It was closed in 1946 and reopened during the Cold War by the US, who used it as a munitions depot. Presently, it served the United States as one of the largest heavy munitions sites in Western Europe. At least, that was the official story. From what Xander had seen since they'd arrived, it looked like Welford also served as a staging area for US intelligence operations in Europe.

Marke kept up a steady stream of words as they walked.

"Following your success taking down Anarchy 99, Gibbons leveraged the Triple-X program into a black-books, Congress-adjacent operation. Triple-X disrupted the status quo, saved millions of lives, and eventually got to the point where Gibbons earned a blank check. Which is a long way of saying, he got you a new ride."

Marke led Xander outside, the sun blinding him for a second. He shielded his eyes, and his vision adjusted to reveal a Boeing C-17 Globemaster III sitting on the runway.

"I liked my old ride better, my GTO," Xander said.

Marke gave him a wry smile and the two of them headed toward the large military transport craft. Despite what he'd said, Xander was impressed. The C-17 was used for transporting troops and cargo around the world, as well as performing tactical and strategic airlift missions. Gibbons must've really impressed the hell out of the bigwigs in Washington in the years since Xander had been gone if they let him have the kind of money a plane like this cost.

Marke resumed her monologue as they walked up a ramp and entered the cargo bay.

"The world got an upgrade since you died, Cage. This bird has on-board drones, anti-air counter-measures, and fuel tanks big enough to circumnavigate the globe three times without ever landing."

Marke paused to remove her coat and handed it to a nearby soldier. Today, she wore a stark black suit instead of the white he'd seen her in earlier. Xander wondered what the woman had against colors. Maybe he'd have to pick up a few tie-dyed T-shirts for her. Marke started toward the stairwell that led to the C-17's upper level, but she stopped and turned back to look at Xander.

"You can check your beloved coat. I promise no one will dare steal it. Of course, I can't guarantee it won't get up and walk away on its own." She raised her voice to call out orders to the crew. "Wheels up in ten, boys, which means you're already seven minutes behind."

Marke mounted the stairs and started up them as everyone scurried to get back to work and make sure the C-17 was ready to take off when she wanted and not a second later. Xander caught the eye of the nearest crewmember.

"She always this fun or only on special occasions?"

Xander followed Marke up into the C-17's Command Center. The interior of the craft was jam-packed with the latest NSA tech, all the toys Xander might've wished for when he was fourteen years old. Hell, he'd like to play with some of this shit now. Everywhere he looked, he saw screens streaming data and more controls than a thousand game consoles put together. Techs sat at workstations, fingers flying across consoles with the speed and dexterity of master musicians pushing their instruments to the limit and beyond.

"Suit, you gotta be kidding me," Xander said as he took it all in. "This is impressive. No wonder our country's a trillion dollars in debt. Do you really need all this gadgetry to catch the bad guys? You could just use some Xander swag."

"Oh, we don't *need* any of it," Marke said with a grin. "But it makes the catching a hell of a lot more fun."

"Xander Cage, holy shit! Live and in concert, one night only!"

Xander turned to see a woman coming out of the cockpit and hurrying toward them. She was a pretty brunette with wide-lens glasses that made her look something like a sexy owl. She wore a white blouse unbuttoned farther than was strictly professional, black slacks, and a simple gold chain around her neck. She spoke at a rapid-fire pace, so fast that Xander had trouble keeping up.

"This is *crazy*, which is saying a lot because I was at Coachella when Guns N' Roses got back together, but this is way cooler. Well, I wasn't actually there, but I heard about it, you know? Oh my god, am I still talking? This is really embarrassing. I'm sorry. When I get started, I just can't stop—I just keep going and going, and then I can't breathe…"

"Don't worry," Xander said, concerned the woman was on the verge of hyperventilating. "It's gonna be okay. Slow down, take deep breaths. I know mouth-to-mouth if necessary, but I don't perform in front of an audience."

Xander wore a black sleeveless top, and the woman reached out and placed trembling fingers on his biceps.

"Oh wow, check out those arms. Are you kidding me with these guns? Look at you, you're like the frickin' Terminator! I'm not talking about the first Terminator, but the second Terminator who was sent to kill the first Terminator, but he was liquid metal like—"

Marke, her patience clearly at an end, interrupted. "Agent Clearidge worked closely with Gibbons. She'll handle support on this operation."

The agent yanked her hands away from Xander's arms as if she were a little girl whose mother had caught her doing something she shouldn't—not in public, anyway.

Xander smiled. "Ah, the new Shavers."

"Yep, that's me. And I bet a guy like you needs a lot of support. What are you, like two-twenty? Two-thirty? Be honest. Two-fifty is like the hard limit for my swing."

Xander laughed. "Oh, come on. You're clowning me."

"I'm *kidding*! It's not like I have a safe word or anything. Kumquat. I don't ever think about stuff like that. Seriously, it's kumquat." She winked. "But enough about me. What about you? What's your safe word?"

Xander liked this woman, and he decided to play

along. "Sister, *safe* is not in my dictionary."

"Touché," she said.

"Never had a need for a safe word. And something tells me you never really had a need for one, either."

Marke sighed. Clearly, she wasn't enjoying their comedy routine. "Yes, well if you need anything, Becky can source it within the hour."

"Except any sort of illegal drugs. Those I'll have within fifteen minutes. *Kidding!* You need a fifty of Martian Mean Green, I am *not* the girl to ask." Another wink.

"Okay, so follow me, Cage. I'll introduce you to your ground team. Thanks, Becky."

Marke headed for the stairwell, and Xander followed, but just before he started down, he turned back and gave Becky a serious look. "Kumquat? With a K?"

She gave him a broad smile in return. "C, K, whatever."

Xander smiled, nodded, and started down the stairs. As he descended, he heard Becky speak to the other techs in the Command Center.

"Stay in school, kids. Don't do drugs."

The Globemaster thundered across the tarmac, rose into the air, and disappeared into the clouds. When they were well underway, Marke led Xander back to the cargo bay. The bay was filled with vehicles and boxes of supplies, all fitted with parachutes so they could be airdropped wherever they were needed. Five NSA spec-ops men were getting equipped for the mission, pulling on tactical camo gear. As the men finished their preparations, the team leader—a broad-shouldered, thick-necked, barrel-chested sonofabitch who looked every inch a professional soldier—saw Marke coming and barked an order.

"Boys, let's fall in!"

The men rushed to line up, and as Marke and Xander approached, the leader looked Xander up and down. It was clear from his scowl and pursed lips that he wasn't impressed with what he saw.

"Oh look," the man said, "it's the poster child for Red Bull."

Marke frowned, but otherwise she ignored the comment. "Xander Cage, I'd like you to meet Paul—"

But Xander interrupted her.

"Donovan," he finished. "*Captain* Paul Donovan. I remember you. I saw you on TV. The President gave you a medal. That must've been pretty cool. What was it for, again? You protected a village from terrorists with no reinforcements for a week?"

"Actually, two weeks," Donovan said, "but who's counting, right?"

Marke continued the introductions. "This is Lieutenant Vasquez, Corporal Jones…"

Xander interrupted her once again. "Lieutenant? Corporal? Suit, with heroes like these, what do you need me for? I mean, these guys are the real heroes. Think of what they've seen and done. They must have great stories to tell. I wanna hear all of 'em."

Xander moved down the line of operatives, shaking hands and fist-bumping as he went. When he was finished, he turned around to regard the men.

"But I wonder," he said, "have any of you ever pulled a triple no-hander on a BMX bike?"

"We don't play on bikes," Donovan said, his tone cold.

"Okay, but surely at least one of you must have carved out an R4 on a snowboard with an avalanche on your tail?"

Donovan's eyes narrowed and his jaw clenched. "We're soldiers, not slackers."

"Really? Not even you? You look like a shredder to me." Xander addressed the other men as he moved toward a set of controls mounted on the cargo bay wall, close to where Marke was standing. "Any of you guys ever HALO jumped over Eastern Europe using only a standard-issue armor deployment parachute?"

The men looked confused, but Donovan had had enough.

"No, because *we're* not all jacked up on Mountain Dew and Red Bull." Donovan turned to Marke. "Where'd you find this clown? Is he for real?"

"Well, guess there's a first time for everything," Xander said.

Xander slapped a button on the control console and the cargo bay door opened. A windstorm erupted in the bay, catching a drogue chute and pulling it out of the plane. The drogue chute, in turn, activated an extraction chute attached to a jeep. That chute filled with wind and yanked the vehicle along the cargo deployment ramp. As the jeep rolled toward the open door, all five operatives, including Donovan, were swept off their feet by the wind. Xander held onto a support bar with one hand, and he grabbed hold of Marke with the other, preventing her from being pulled out with the spec-ops team. As the jeep rolled out the bay door, Donovan and his men grabbed for it, and then both vehicle and men tumbled away into the open air. A few seconds later, the wind died down as the pressure equalized, and Xander let Marke go.

The normally unflappable woman seemed absolutely shocked at what he'd done.

"You dumb cowboy!" she shouted. "What did you just do? I don't believe this shit!"

"If they're as highly trained as I think they are, they'll catch hold of the jeep and ride it down together. But as heroic and altruistic as those GI Joes seem, I can't have monkeys watching my back."

Marke sighed. "I know I'm going to regret asking this, but who *would* you trust?"

Xander smiled.

4

Back in the C-17's Command Center, Xander called up a file on a workstation computer screen. Several paragraphs of text appeared, along with a picture of a heavily tattooed woman with short green hair, dressed in a black sleeveless tee and leather pants.

"Adele Wolff," he said. "Triggerman, sniper, overwatch. You name it, she does it. And she does it better than anyone else in the world."

Marke leaned closer to the screen so she could read the text that accompanied the photo. "Says here she's also wanted by the FBI on counts of felony destruction, assault, possession—"

"So you were never a teenager? Besides, she did the time."

Marke turned to Xander and raised a questioning eyebrow. "She has seven outstanding warrants with the justice department."

"No, that's not what I mean. She wrecked her BMX on a two story, broke twenty-seven bones. She was horizontal for two years."

Becky's eyes widened. "*Two years?*"

Xander nodded. "Believe me, she did the time. After she recovered, she couldn't ride anymore—not at the level she used to, anyway. She was bored out of her mind, and lucky for us, she picked up a sniper rifle."

"And some green hair dye," Marke said with obvious disapproval.

"Let's just say she's the kind of person who turns a hobby into an obsession."

AFRICA, THE SERENGETI

The setting sun hung low over the Masai Mara National Reserve, painting the clouds with a spectacular combination of pastel colors—yellows, oranges, pinks, and blues. The trees in the distance became stark silhouettes, lonely sentinels prepared to watch over the land as night descended. But Adele knew there would be no one standing guard over the grasslands here this night.

She crawled through the tall grass, wearing a rifle case backpack, senses alive and alert, intricate tattoos acting like camouflage. The Serengeti was one of the most beautiful places she'd ever been, but more than that, she felt at home here, moving silently through the brush as if she was born to it. In her own way, she was an apex predator, and tonight she was on the hunt.

She caught sight of a lion sitting on a kopje, a rocky outcropping. The big cat was stretched out near the edge of the kopje, head resting on his paws, eyes closed. Lions were the only cats on earth that formed close social bonds with others of their kind and regularly hunted in groups. But Adele saw no sign of any other lions in the vicinity. Maybe this lion had decided he needed some "me" time and had taken a break from his pride to enjoy a quiet snooze on a comfy rock that had been warmed by the sun all day. Or maybe he simply preferred being on his own, with no one to answer to and no one to tie him down.

Adele smiled. I know just how you feel, big guy.

One of the things that Adele appreciated the most about the Serengeti was that it was the last place on earth where big mammals lived. Most people didn't realize that these animals were the remnants of prehistoric creatures that had gone extinct throughout the rest of the world, that this place was like a glimpse into another time, in many ways a better time, before humans had come on the scene and started fucking everything up. A time when life was much simpler, when it was hunt or starve, kill or be killed. The only real question was where you fit into the ecosystem—were you predator or prey? Adele figured it all depended on circumstance: sometimes you were the hunter and sometimes you were the hunted. And tonight the lion was the one being hunted.

The Masai Mara was world-renowned for its large lion population, and here—as in eighty percent of the Serengeti in Tanzania and Kenya—the big cats were legally protected. But just because it was illegal to hunt and kill lions in the Mara didn't mean that people didn't do it. If you were smart, careful, and above all sneaky as hell, you could get away with it.

And that's why humans are the most dangerous predators of all, Adele thought. *Because we don't play fair.*

She slipped off her backpack, opened it, and began assembling her sniper rifle. When she was finished, she lay prone in the grass and put her right eye to the scope. The image was blurry at first, and she made a simple adjustment, and then the lion came into focus. *Honey, you're absolutely gorgeous,* she thought.

She gazed at the lion for several more seconds before repositioning her rifle. Now the scope showed three men approaching the lion from the other side of the kopje. All three were armed with rifles, and they moved slowly and silently so as not to alert the big cat.

Adele's upper lip curled in disgust. *Fucking poachers.*

She aimed, drew in a breath, held it for a second, and then squeezed the trigger as she exhaled. *Thip!* She shot the first poacher in the leg. *Thip!* She shot the second in the arm. *Thip!* She shot the third in the ear. The silencer on her rifle had muffled the sound of her shots and she'd fired in rapid succession, so the poachers had no idea what was happening until they were all hit. The three men went down, dropping their weapons as they fell. They also cried out in pain, and the lion's eyes snapped open.

Adele smiled and began disassembling her rifle.

Several moments later she was walking through the brush, weapon safely stowed in her pack, when she felt a phone buzz in her pocket. Surprised, she stopped and answered it.

"No way," she said in an Australian accent. "*No one has this number.*"

"*So why'd you answer?*" said a familiar male voice, one she hadn't heard in years.

She grinned from ear to ear. "Well, when a dead man learns how to use a phone, it piques my curiosity."

"*What are you up to these days?*" Xander asked.

"Me? I'm evening the odds."

She started walking again as behind her the lion roared and the poachers screamed.

Xander closed Adele's file and brought another up on the screen. This one belonged to a tall fedora-wearing, plaid-shirted man in his forties, with a thick black beard and a slightly crazed look in his eyes.

"Tennyson Torch," Xander said. "Stunt driver out of Chicago. Hundred-ninety-eight lifetime crashes. He's walked away from all of 'em."

Marke read a line from Tennyson's profile aloud.

"Acute psychosis and severe paranoia brought on by massive head trauma."

"He's not fast," Xander said, "but he gets you where you need to go."

CHICAGO

Tennyson climbed behind the wheel of his Chrysler sedan, the car creaking under his weight. Not because he was fat, but because the vehicle's suspension had seen better days. He closed the door and started the engine. The car might be old, but its motor sounded strong and sure. Just like him, right? A little worn on the outside, but inside, still raring to go. He pulled a plastic mouth guard from his shirt pocket, placed it between his teeth, and then gripped the steering wheel with both hands, and gazed through the windshield and out into the street. Visualization was the key to a successful stunt. The more times you pictured what you intended to accomplish—*experienced* it on a mental level—the greater your chances for pulling it off. So that's what he did now. He ran through the scenario once, twice, three times. But he stopped there. Four times was too much. Four times and you were likely to jinx yourself. After all, in Mandarin Chinese, the pronunciation of the word representing the number *four* was similar to the pronunciation of the word for *death*. Coincidence? Tennyson knew there was no such thing.

Go time, he thought.

He put the car in drive, pulled away from the curb, and jammed his foot down on the accelerator. It was nighttime, and the traffic was lighter on the street now than during the day, granting him an unobstructed pathway to his goal: an ATM vestibule at the end of the block. Tennyson gripped the steering wheel tighter and bit down on his mouth guard as the car roared toward the ATM. As he always did just before impact, he closed his eyes. He heard the shattering sound as the vehicle crashed through double-reinforced glass, but he didn't hear the car smash into the ATM. He didn't feel it, either. For an instant, everything went black and silent. He wasn't afraid. This happened to him during every crash. He never knew if it was because he was momentarily stunned or if this crash was the one that was finally going to make him take the off-ramp to the afterlife. Not knowing was all part of the fun.

Tennyson returned to awareness as he fell out of the car. Evidently the driver's-side door had sprung open during the crash. But that wasn't the only machine that had opened. Amidst the smoke and debris, twenty-dollar bills rained down around him. He was rich!

Laughing, he rose to his feet, leaned over, kissed the car's roof in thanks, and then began snatching money out of the air and stuffing it down his pants and shirt. When he figured he couldn't carry any more, he turned and stepped off the curb, only to see an FBI SWAT team waiting for him, guns at the ready. Before he could react, a pair of officers charged Tennyson, grabbed hold of him, and slammed him down on the vehicle's crumpled hood.

"It was like that when I got here," Tennyson said.

The next file belonged to a young Asian man wearing a hoodie, black hair buzzed close to his scalp.

"Nicky Zhou," Xander said. "Everybody calls him Nicks. If you have a problem and he's around, you don't have a problem."

Marke frowned. "I don't get it. What's that mean? He have training?"

"No."

Her frown deepened. "Any sort of field experience?"

Xander shook his head. "Not really."

NEW YORK CITY

The underground club was called Valhalla, not that there was any sign outside to let people know that. If you were one of the people who were supposed to know the club was here, then you *knew*. If you didn't, then you were shit out of luck. And even if you did know about Valhalla, that didn't mean you could get in. A veritable mob of people crowded the sidewalk outside the club, many of them pushing and shoving to get through the door, but precious few could make it past the pair of bouncers on duty—a six-foot-seven, 280-pound, shaven-headed, red-bearded, pierced and tatted monster, and a scary five-foot-five dude who had muscles on his muscles, a thousand-yard stare, and teeth that looked as if they'd been filed to points.

Unfortunately, Nicks—sunglasses on, wearing a hoodie under a black leather jacket—was one of the people on the wrong side of the rope tonight. But he was patient. He could wait for the right opportunity to present itself, and fortunately for him, it looked like it was on its way right now. For the last several minutes, he'd been watching a particularly edgy-looking guy who'd been giving the bouncers the stink-eye. The man wore only black jeans and a pair of boots, but he was covered with intricately detailed tattoos on every inch of his exposed flesh, including his face, so he looked not only as if he were completely dressed, but as if he were also wearing a mask. Tatman, as Nicks thought of him, was bouncing up and down with barely constrained energy, and Nicks guessed the man was psyching himself up to make a go at the door. He let out a series of short breaths—*huh-huh-huh*—and then he ran toward the club's entrance.

Give 'em hell, Tatman! Nicks thought.

When the crowd saw what the man was doing, they let out raucous cheers, but Gossamer grabbed hold of Tatman and lifted him off his feet as easily as if the man weighed no more than a toddler.

Gossamer seemed more amused than angry. "Look,

man, you want to get into this party, you either gotta break some bones or break some records."

Tatman swore as he thrashed in Gossamer's arms, and the man's exertions drew the other guard's attention. *That* was what Nicks had been waiting for. While the second bouncer was momentarily distracted, he slipped under the rope and hurried through the entrance before either bouncer could notice. He was in!

Valhalla's interior was a riot of sight and sound, a relentless sensory onslaught so overwhelming that it felt as if his consciousness might flip the off switch to protect itself from the tsunami of input. Nicks, of course, loved it. In Norse mythology, Valhalla was the sacred realm where the spirits of dead warriors spent eternity in glorious battle. This Valhalla was a paradise for warriors too. Not those who fought with sword or spear, but rather those whose weapons of choice were bikes, boards, boats, skis, parachutes, and hang gliders. Music thumped and lights flashed as skaters and bikers took turns on a ramp, tricking over the bar, while a sexy MC amped the crowd up from the stage.

"You're gonna have to get louder than that!" the woman shouted. "Okay, guys, are you ready for the main event?"

The crowd roared, and Nicks could feel the floor vibrate beneath his feet. He grinned. Now *this* was what he was talking about!

He saw superstar athletes in every direction he looked,

and he began to make his way through the crowd, fist-bumping perfect strangers as if they were long-lost friends as he went. As he passed a Who's Who of the most dangerous sports in the world, their stats ran through his mind.

Nyjah Huston. X-Games Gold Medalist. *Thrasher Magazine* Skater of the Year. 1.6 million followers.

He gave Nyjah a fist bump and kept going.

Nina Buitrago, aka The Burrito. BMX Metro JAM Champion. Broken jaw. Reconstructed shoulder. Quote: "Life is better on two wheels."

Dani Windhausen, aka Dani Lightningbolt. BMX Ripper. Broken ankle, broken wrist, shattered knee. Quote: "Living the dream!"

Jamie Anderson. Snowboard shredder. Olympic Gold Medalist. Slopestyle World Record Holder. Broken collar bone.

He stopped to give Jamie a hug, whispered a quick joke that was extremely filthy, and she laughed and punched him on the shoulder. Grinning, he moved on, heading in the general direction of the stage. He felt an itching sensation on the back of his neck, which he took as a warning, and he glanced over his shoulder to see that the big bouncer was tracking him through the crowd. Unconcerned, Nicks looked forward once again and kept moving, passing more of the awesome and the famous as he went.

Chad Kerley. BMX Freestyle. X-Games Gold. Pro at

17. Fractured jaw. Six teeth removed. Quote: "I could ride from New York to China."

Nicks saw a pair of security guards making their way through the crowd toward him, and he knew that the bouncer had alerted them to his presence. He continued on, weaving his way through the crowd, using the people for cover.

A beautiful brunette walked toward Nicks, probably on her way to the bar or the restroom, he thought. He recognized her, of course: *Roberta Mancino.* Skydiver. BASE jumper. Wingsuit flyer. Daredevil. International Supermodel.

Nicks knew he shouldn't, but he couldn't resist. He removed his sunglasses, stepped up to Roberta, and gave her a quick kiss. At first she looked upset, but then he smiled sheepishly and shrugged, and she laughed, shook her head, and moved on.

The bouncer and the security guards were closing in on him. He'd better haul ass if he didn't want to get tossed out on it. As he drew closer to the stage, his mouth dropped open when he saw who was standing there, waiting for the next set to begin. *Tony Hawk.* The Birdman. Nine-time X-Games Champion. First inductee to Skateboarding Hall of Fame. Vert God. King among men.

Then he imagined what his own stats might be: *Nicky "Nicks" Zhou.* Just some guy. No known records. No known injuries. No known *anything*.

He laughed and kept moving toward the stage. As he did, the MC shouted, "You ready for the main event?"

The crowd cheered.

"I don't know," the MC said, sounding doubtful. "It doesn't sound like you're ready…"

The crowd screamed, louder and louder, stomping their feet so hard that the entire building shook. The MC grinned, clearly enjoying bringing the crowd to a fever pitch. The crowd knew she was working them, and they ate it up.

"Maybe I should just tell him to skip his set tonight," she said. "How 'bout that?"

Louder, louder, louder…

"Maybe we should all just go home…"

Louder yet, the noise so intense now that it rolled over Nicks like a physical force. Without anywhere else to go, Nicks hopped up onto the stage.

The crowd went silent then, confused, and then the MC shouted, "Show him the love! Give it up for… The Hood!"

The crowd exploded into thunderous applause, and Nick pulled up his hoodie face mask and turned around. Spotlights moved to focus on him, giving the crowd its first good look at the Hood's "face"—a bald, somewhat alien-looking visage with shadow-shrouded eyes. In the audience, the bouncer and the security gazed up at him, confused. Nicks thought about flipping them the bird, but then decided against it. The guys were just doing their jobs, right?

The MC approached Nicks and handed him the microphone. She gave him a peck on the cheek—or rather, on the mask *over* his cheek—and winked.

"What took you so long?" she said.

"You know me. I like to make my entrance."

Nicks jumped behind a set of turntables and dropped a massive beat. Impossibly, the crowd's cheers became even louder, and Nicks wouldn't have been surprised if the sound caused the building to collapse. *Talk about bringing the house down,* he thought. New stats flashed through his mind then:

The Hood. 100,000,000 streams. 100,000,000 likes. 100,000,000 followers. Quote: "I don't party. I live."

"So what's his specialty?" Marke said, clearly irritated. "What's he do?"

Xander smiled. "Mostly he's just fun to have around."

RAF WELFORD, BERKSHIRE

Xander stood in the Globemaster's cargo bay as three Suburbans pulled onto the runway. The bay door was open, and Xander watched as the vehicles stopped at the rear of the plane and their passengers disembarked. He grinned.

"Look who it is," he said. "The good, the badass, and the

completely insane. Now *this* is a team I can get behind."

Adele, Nicks, and Tennyson walked up the ramp to greet him.

"Read a rumor on PsiOps you weren't really dead," Tennyson said.

"Did you?" Xander said.

Tennyson looked back and forth, as if to check if anyone was listening. "How many lives you got?" he said, his voice low. He sounded as if he seriously believed Xander had somehow been resurrected from the dead.

"Depends on who's counting. Good to see you, Tennyson."

Xander gave the man a hug. When the two men pulled apart, Nicks moved in to snag a hug of his own.

"You still partying?" Xander said when Nicks stepped back.

"Always," Nicks said with a grin.

Adele came forward then.

"Ho, so you're counting lives now? How many do you owe me?" she asked. "Two, three?"

"I'm not counting Sri Lanka," Xander said.

"How you gonna *not* count Sri Lanka? One, two, Sri Lanka."

"I count this way," Xander said. "One, two…" He turned the back of his hand toward her and held up the first three fingers. "Read between the lines."

"I swear, you—" She drew her fist back as if she

intended to punch him, but instead she laughed and went in for a hug instead.

"Oh, see? This is what I miss," Xander said.

Xander asked Becky to come down to the cargo bay and show his friends some of the cool toys they were going to have a chance to play with. Becky joined them and immediately began opening equipment lockers containing a cache of high-tech gear and weapons, as excited to show them off as the others were to see them. Tennyson and Nicks stood in awe, while Adele stepped forward and began pulling everything out to examine it. Xander stood back and watched with amusement while his friends acted like kids in a candy store—and a very *lethal* candy store, at that.

Becky removed a box with a pair of metallic gloves, and Nicks gave a low whistle when he saw them. "Whoa, I'm gonna need a minute. This is mine!"

"These are my favorite, too," Becky said. "They're called Exo-Gloves. They're DARPA's new ground combat technology. Pneumatic pistons drive the gears and quadruple the speed and power of your punches."

Tennyson picked up a metal box from a nearby steel table a little too roughly, and the sides fell away. An alarmed look came over Becky's face, and she thrust the box containing the Exo-Gloves into Nicks's hands and rushed toward Tennyson.

"No, no, no, no! That's a multi-stage signal disruptor. It's very, very breakable." She took the device from Tennyson and gently put it back on the table.

Tennyson looked around, then leaned in close to Becky and whispered, "Can you tell me the real reason behind the crash of Pan Am 103 over Lockerbie?"

"No," she whispered back.

Tennyson frowned. "You can't or you won't?"

"Yes," she said, and then added, "Aliens."

Tennyson's eyes narrowed, and he looked at her for a long moment. Finally he said, "You're *one* of them, aren't you?"

Becky smiled. "If I was, I wouldn't tell you now, would I?"

Nicks had put the box containing the Exo-Gloves on the floor, removed one, slipped it on, and now he started air-boxing with it. Becky saw what he was doing, and she turned away from Tennyson, no longer smiling.

"Hey, easy there, Rocky," she said, sounding nervous. "Those things have enough force to—"

Nicks's movements somehow activated the glove, and the pistons ratcheted back and slammed forward, causing the glove to slam into a bulkhead with tremendous force.

"—punch a hole in the frickin' plane," Becky finished.

Startled, Nicks stepped back and looked at the damage he'd caused to the bulkhead. "I can fix it," he said.

"Don't worry about it," Becky said. "It's not like there's

anything expensive here. Just keep screwing around. What could possibly go wrong?"

Nicks removed the glove and handed it back to Becky. "But that's my style, though."

She gave Nicks an uneasy smile. "Good. I'm glad. Good, good." She returned the glove to its box and then put the box back in the locker it had come from. Then she noticed Adele assembling a next-gen sniper rifle on the table. Becky started toward Adele, panic on her face.

"I'd really rather you didn't…" Becky began, but then she trailed off as she watched Adele's hands moving with smooth, confident precision. "Oh, you actually know what you're doing. That's refreshing."

Adele didn't look up as she worked. "That's what she said."

"Speaking of what people said…" Becky stepped next to Adele and lowered her voice. "You and Xander seem… *close*. How did you two meet?"

Adele finished putting the rifle together, and she lifted it into firing position, getting a feel for the weapon. "My back was against the wall, two bullets in my leg, and I was surrounded by insurgents. Then Xander Cage comes out of the smoke, machine gun in one arm, rocket launcher strapped to his back."

"Wow!" Becky said, wide-eyed. "That's frickin' *amazing*! Only Xander Cage could pull that off. Where was it? Syria? Lebanon? Afghanistan?"

"Nuketown," Adele said as she looked through the rifle's scope. "*Call of Duty.*"

Becky frowned. "Like the game?"

Adele lowered the rifle and looked at Becky, her expression deadly serious. "Like the way of life."

Xander grinned. This mission was going to be *fun*.

The Globemaster took off not long after that, and while Adele, Nicks, and Tennyson were getting a tour of the Command Center, Xander and Becky were alone in the cargo bay. Xander had his shirt off and he was trying on an armored vest, attempting to get the fit just right, but he couldn't quite—

He heard Becky come up behind him, felt her reach around his body.

"You, um, need to… fix this strap. Here, I'll do it. I just need to get a little closer to see. Not a lot of light here."

She pushed close to Xander and tightened the straps of the vest around his torso. When the vest was snug, he turned around to face her. She didn't back away, but she swallowed nervously.

"So what are you?" Xander said. "My handler?"

She reached out to finish the vest's upper straps and cinched his torso tight, the motion a little more forceful than strictly necessary.

"Whatever you need," she said, her voice throaty. "I can handle anything. I got a firm grip. Or so I've been told."

Xander raised his left arm. Becky's hand was clamped around his wrist.

"I can see that," he said.

"Sorry." She let go of his wrist and took a step back. "There's something I should tell you."

Xander raised an eyebrow. "Oh?"

"It's nothing like *that*," she said. ". Just so we're clear: I don't get off the plane. Don't even ask. It's in my contract."

"You know, outside is where all the fun is."

Becky spoke fast then, even faster than she usually did. "Fun scares me. People scare me. Guns scare me. People with guns scare me. If I'm scared, I can't do my job. And if I can't do my job, people die. And if everyone dies, who am I tech supporting? Literally no one. But I'll make sure to keep you safe."

A tension-filled silence fell between them then, one that Xander finally broke with a laugh.

"Keeping *me* safe ain't easy."

He took off her glasses. She was beautiful with them on, but without them—without the barriers between her and the world—she gained an added vulnerability that was almost irresistible.

She stepped closer once more and leaned forward, as if she might kiss him. But instead she said, "Challenge accepted."

* * *

By unspoken agreement, Xander and his team had made the cargo bay their headquarters, so when it came time for Marke to brief them, she did it there. Everyone gathered around a monitor mounted on a wall, and Becky brought up images of the thieves who'd broken into the CIA installation and stolen Pandora's Box.

"I'll make this easy for you," Marke said. "These four assholes: very bad guys. Pandora's Box: very bad thing. We'll land in Manila, and you will requisition your own transportation to the island where they're currently hiding out."

"Yo," Nicks said, "why don't we just nuke the bitch from orbit and call it a day?"

Marke bristled at Nicks's less-than-professional tone, but she said, "Pandora's Box is one of a kind, and it must be recovered intact."

Tennyson scowled. "Why? What's it do? Brainwave scrambler?" He thought for a moment, then nodded. "Yeah, it's a brainwave scrambler."

Marke tightened her lips in irritation. "It killed Gibbons is all you need to know. The rest is classified."

Adele tilted her head back and sniffed a couple times. "What's that smell? Oh, I know." She lowered her head and fixed her gaze on Marke. "Same old shit, different suit."

Marke responded with barely restrained anger. "You think a dog knows how to work a Frisbee? Master says fetch and the bitch listens."

Adele held her newly acquired rifle. In fact, she'd barely let go of it since putting it together. She now slotted a round into the rifle, raised it into firing position, and looked through the scope, the weapon's barrel pointed directly at Marke. Marke held her ground, but it was clear from the uncertain expression on her face that she wasn't sure how to react.

"I know that game," Adele said, "except usually I'm the master." She lowered the rifle and looked at Marke as if truly seeing her for the first time. "You know, I think you'd look really hot with a Frisbee in your mouth."

"I'm not here to play," Marke said, regaining some of her composure. "The point is, you are all *my* soldiers now."

"I'm a baller, not a soldier," Nicks said.

"Oh, *hell* no," Adele said.

Xander had remained quiet up to this point, but now he was getting pissed. "I dropped *your* soldiers over Eastern Europe."

Adele jerked her chin toward Marke. "Why'd you leave Lassie behind?"

Marke's eyes blazed with fury. "This is *my* operation, and you *will* listen to me!"

This situation is about to go seriously off the rails, Xander thought. "Guys, come on. Fall back."

Marke didn't say anything for a moment, but when she finally spoke, most of the anger had left her voice. "Yeah, take a breather."

Xander's team glanced at him and then walked away, pointedly not looking in Marke's direction. When the three of them were out of earshot, Xander turned to Marke.

"You're *really* good at motivational speaking," he said.

"I try," she said with a trace of bitterness.

"I should take lessons from you."

She looked at him for a moment. "You couldn't afford them."

"Remember, you *asked* me to help you," he said.

"Maybe so," she allowed, "but I didn't invite your circus. Train your animals."

There were a lot of things Xander wanted to say to Marke at that moment, but he figured it would be wiser to keep his mouth shut. So he turned his back on Marke without saying anything and followed after his team. As he left, he heard Becky say, "But other than that, Mrs. Lincoln, how was the play?"

5

Xander walked along the harbor, keeping his eye out for a suitable boat that he could "requisition." He wanted something reliable, not big or flashy, but fast enough that if they needed to outrun someone, they could. After a while, a bowrider moored at a slip in the marina caught his eye. It was an older model, but it had obviously been well maintained. Bowriders were the most popular sports boats, so it wouldn't draw much attention, and they had abundant seating in the open bow so there would be plenty of room for the team. They had sterndrive power, and hulls with more of a V-shape than other boats. This allowed them to turn sharper, especially at high speed, and handle rougher water.

It was perfect.

The owner, a Filipino man in his sixties, was onboard the bowrider when Xander approached the slip. Xander hailed him in Filipino, and the man smiled and waved him aboard his vessel. Xander spent a few minutes making small talk with the man—whose name was Danilo. They discussed the weather, the tides, and the fishing in the area, and Xander made sure to comment on Danilo's efforts to keep the bowrider in such good shape. After a time, Xander came to the point: he wanted to buy the man's boat. At first Danilo was taken aback by the offer, but he recovered his composure and politely declined Xander's offer. Xander then removed an envelope filled with cash from inside his coat and tried to hand it to Danilo, but the man waved him off.

"She's not for sale, sorry," he said in Filipino.

Xander opened his coat to reveal ten more envelopes pinned to the inside lining.

"How about now?" he asked.

Danilo's eyes went wide, and slowly his mouth stretched into a wide grin.

Best friends now, Xander thought, and he smiled.

They waited until night to head out to sea, Tennyson piloting the craft. Xander figured it would be safe enough for the man to drive. After all, what was there for him to crash into on the open ocean? Then again, this *was* Tennyson. The man could probably crash a boat by colliding with an unlucky shrimp. Nicks sat next to Tennyson, probably because he wanted to keep an eye on the man to make sure he didn't do anything crazy that would get the rest of them killed. That left Xander alone with Adele, which worked just fine for him. They stood in the bow, gazing out past the bowrider's lights to the dark waves beyond. Adele's arms were around him, and the spray felt good on Xander's body. Not as good as Adele's embrace, though. In his turbulent life, Xander had learned to appreciate moments like this, because you never knew if they would be among your last.

They remained like that for a while, silent, but eventually Adele spoke.

"You know what's a long time?" she asked. "Seven years."

Xander had known this was coming. Better now than later, he supposed. "Yeah, but I thought about you every single day."

"I don't need some corny Xander line."

"What's corny about it?" He didn't admit that it was a line, because while on one level it was, on another it was the absolute truth. After faking his death, he couldn't afford to stay in any one place—or in any one relationship—too long. Because of this, he'd been with many women, but he'd only given pieces of himself to a precious few. And Adele had been one of them.

Adele changed the subject, letting him off the hook. "I've been riding again. Three years now. Not like before, of course, not yet. But maybe someday."

"That's good. Everything's better on two wheels."

"Everything's better with you around. Big teddy bear." She snuggled closer to him, and Xander put an arm around her.

"You always took better care of me than anyone else," he said.

"Think I don't know that? That's why I'm here."

"You always have my back."

She looked at him for a moment, eyes searching his, seeking what, though, he didn't know. Finally, with a deadpan expression, she said, "You're the bane of my existence."

Xander laughed.

On the bridge behind them, they heard Nicks raise his voice.

"You're so full of shit, it's comin' out your ears," he said.

They approached a web of wooden posts, and Tennyson slowed the bowrider to maneuver around them. They were getting close to the island.

"It's true," Tennyson said. "I've seen the documents."

"You *really* think the CIA spent countless man-hours and millions of taxpayer dollars to what? Break up Kim and Kanye?"

"Do you think I *like* knowing this stuff? I'd rather get a good night's sleep with you and the rest of the sheep."

Nicks sighed. "If someone shoots at you tonight, please remind me not to stand in their way."

Adele made a face, irritated by their silly conversation.

"Yo, Real Housewives of Dipshit County," she called back to them, "shut up or I'll shoot you myself."

As they drew closer to the posts, Xander saw armed pirates balancing atop them. They raised their weapons and laser sights flickered on, catching the team in a lattice of crimson red. Adele leaned close to Xander and spoke quietly.

"I count twenty-one guns," she said.

"Bet they think that makes it a fair fight," Xander said.

One of the sentries let out a sharp whistle, and another fired a green flare up into the sky. The signal was unmistakable: safe to pass. Despite the team being given the go-ahead, the pirates tracked them with their laser sights as they passed. Tennyson piloted the bowrider toward a pier. Numerous campfires lit the beach, and a series of torches illuminated massive temple ruins on the hill beyond. *Can't have a secret pirate island without ruins*, Xander thought. *Ten points for style.*

A woman flanked by armed guards waited for them at the end of the pier, most of them holding electric lanterns to provide light.

"You wanna party here, you have to pay the toll," the woman said.

Farther back on the pier, hidden by shadow, Xander noticed another woman. She watched as they approached, and then she was gone, melted into the darkness as if she'd never been there in the first place.

Interesting, Xander thought.

Tennyson cut the bowrider's engines and pulled the boat up next to their welcoming committee. The guards raised their guns and trained them on Xander and the others. The men were all of a type that Xander knew well. Rough and dirty, gazes cold and unfeeling, the kind of men who would kill you in an instant and never lose a wink of sleep over it. He appreciated people like this. They were what they were and didn't pretend to be anything else. He didn't like them, and he sure as hell didn't admire them, but you knew where you stood with men like these. And that meant you could deal with them—*if* you spoke the right language.

One of the guards tossed them a line. Xander caught it and tied the end to a cleat. This didn't mean they were welcome, yet. It only meant that they could begin negotiating.

A man stepped forward, accompanied by three extremely attractive women. *Looks like he's got himself a traveling harem,* Xander thought. The man carried no weapon, but each of his companions did, and from the frosty look in their eyes, Xander figured they knew how to use them. The man was tall, lean, tanned, and scraggle-bearded, and although he smiled, his gaze was calculating as he sized up the new arrivals.

Xander nodded to Tennyson, and he began to offload a heavy trunk. Xander, Adele, and Nicks disembarked then. None of them were carrying weapons, not even Adele, who clearly wasn't happy about it.

Xander smiled at the bearded man, whom he took to be the island's leader—or at least as much of a leader as a lawless place could have. "We just happened to be floating around the South Pacific, and I heard this was the perfect place for me and my crew to lay low for a couple of days, no questions asked."

The bearded man kept smiling, but his eyes remained wary. "*Mi casa es su casa, amigo*—if the price is right."

"I've got some of the best hardware in the South Pacific," Xander said. "Tennyson!" he ordered.

Tennyson carried the trunk over to Xander and the pirate leader and put it down in front of them. It was heavy, and it slipped out of his hands and fell the last several inches, slamming onto the wood with significant force. *That* got the leader's attention, and his smile took on a greedy edge. Xander gestured to the trunk. *Help yourself, amigo.* The leader stepped forward and opened the trunk to reveal the weapons Xander and the others had stolen from the Globemaster.

The pirate leader practically drooled as he spoke, his gaze fixed on the weapons. "Thirty percent off the top gets you our finest hospitality package."

"Thirty percent?" Xander said, sounding incredulous. "Do I get to take the girls home for the weekend for that? Honestly, I heard ten."

That broke the spell the sight of the weapons had cast on the pirate leader. He looked at Xander, his eyes wide with disbelief. "*Ay, dios mio!* Ten percent? *Esta loco.* You musta been aiming for the other lawless, uncharted island down the block. Don't worry about it, happens all the time. Here's what you gonna do: turn around, get on your boat, and kiss my ass. Okay?"

Xander turned to Tennyson. "What do you think?" Without waiting for the man's reply, Xander said, "Yeah, you're right." He turned back to the leader. "Eighteen percent."

"Eighteen percent?" The pirate acted as if Xander had just personally insulted him. "You think we at a flea market in the hood? You think we sellin' broken TVs and fake watches?"

"Okay, my final offer. Twenty-two and a half."

The leader looked at Xander as if he was crazy. "*Twenty-two and a half*? How you gonna do a half?"

"Twenty-two of these puppies. And a half."

Xander bent down, took a rifle from the trunk, gripped it with both hands, gritted his teeth, and snapped the weapon in half. He then handed one of the pieces to the leader.

The man took the half-a-gun and looked at it for a long moment. The women who'd accompanied him tightened their grip on their weapons, as did the other pirates on the pier. One word from the leader, and Xander knew the bullets would start flying. The tension wasn't quite as intense a rush as BASE-jumping from Meru Peak in the Himalayas, but it wasn't bad, either. The spy game did have its side benefits.

Finally the pirate smiled and stepped forward to hug Xander. When he stepped back, he said, "I like you. You are my type of guy. Enjoy the party."

The man, who introduced himself as Lazarus, ordered a couple of other pirates to take the trunk onto the island. As the men hurried to obey, Xander stepped over to Tennyson and softly said, "Stay on the boat. No matter what."

Tennyson nodded, and then Xander called for Adele and Nicks to accompany him. Nicks brought Xander his coat, and he shrugged it on. Lazarus returned and pointed down the pier. Music and laughter was audible in the distance—the party Lazarus had mentioned.

Lazarus gazed out at the horizon. "Only an hour 'til dawn." Then he looked at Xander and frowned. "Hey, aren't you that guy from the Xander Zone videos?"

Xander smiled. "You know, I get that a lot."

The party turned out to be held in the temple ruins, of course. As Xander, Adele, and Nicks walked up the steps, they heard diffuse music bleeding out of the building. Xander and Adele got their weapons off the bowrider before leaving the pier. Xander carried a pistol tucked into his pants against the small of his back, while Adele carried her hi-tech sniper rifle in a backpack. Nicks had passed on a weapon. *Not my style,* he'd said. As they climbed the steps, Xander scrutinized the temple more closely. He was no expert, but the architecture of the temple looked Thai to him. He guessed it was centuries old, at least, and he wondered what the people who built this place and held it sacred would think if they could see the use it was being put to now. Somehow, he didn't think they'd be pleased.

He turned to Adele. "You're my eyes in the sky, like always. Find yourself a nice perch. There's a sail right over there."

A beached catamaran lay off to the side of the temple. Adele gave Xander a nod, jogged over to the boat, drew a knife from her boot, quickly cut away the sail, replaced the knife, and then vaulted up the side of the temple into a tree, swift and silent as a cat. She climbed upward until she found a vantage point that allowed her to see through one of the temple's windows, and then she quickly began fashioning the sail into a rigging to hold her.

Xander turned to Nicks. "You're with me. Gonna show 'em how we do it."

"Hell, yeah," Nicks said.

They continued the rest of the way up the steps to a pair of large wooden doors with metal handles. Xander took hold of them and pulled the doors open, releasing a cacophony of sound. He grinned at Nicks, and then gestured for the man to precede him. It was only fitting that Nicks went in first, since he was a world-class party-master. Nicks gave Xander a bow of thanks, entered, and Xander followed, closing the doors behind him. Inside, sweating bodies were smashed together, drinking, dancing, and grinding to a relentless throbbing beat as a reggaetón singer on a stage rapped in rapid-fire Spanish. The man wore a black cap and leather jacket, and a half-dozen beautiful women danced around him as he performed. At first glance, the temple interior looked like any other club, no different than hundreds of others like it around the world. But Xander knew it had one major difference. The revelers in this club were all extremely dangerous people who would seriously fuck you up just for looking at them wrong.

My kinda place, he thought.

Thanks to Becky, Xander and his team wore tactical bone-conduction earpieces that would allow them to communicate with each other. The devices were the highest of high-tech and almost completely invisible. You had to get real close to someone wearing one to see it, and even then you had to know what you were looking for. Xander tapped his ear to activate the device, and Nicks did the same. *Coulda used these yesterday,* Xander thought. He had no doubt Adele had already activated hers. The last thing she would ever do was allow him to enter a dangerous situation without her being able to see and hear everything he was doing—and he loved her for it.

Xander spoke softly to test the device. "You got this?" he said to Nicks.

Nicks nodded to let Xander know his earpiece was working. He replied just as softly as Xander had spoken. "Just watch me," he said.

Xander and Nicks made their way through the throng of partiers to a bar tended by a gorgeous bikini-clad woman. Xander slipped off his coat and handed it to her.

"Can you keep this behind the bar for me?" he asked.

She smiled, nodded, and took the coat. As she did, Nicks turned around and surveyed the territory.

"This got an Ibiza vibe to it," he said.

"I'm surprised you remember that trip," Xander said. "Don't make me carry you out this time."

Nicks grinned. "No promises."

Now that the bartender had stowed away Xander's coat, she touched his hand and smiled. "What can I get you?" she asked.

He leaned in close and whispered, "A cranberry and club soda, please." He glanced at Nicks, and when he saw the man hadn't heard him, he said, "Make that two."

If the woman thought there was anything odd about his drink selection, she gave no sign. She smiled, nodded, and went to work preparing his order. When she was finished, she handed him the two drinks.

"Thank you," Xander said.

"You're welcome." Her tone made it clear that he was

welcome to more than cranberry juice if he was interested.

Xander turned to Nicks and put one of the drinks into his hand. Nicks—still taking everything in—brought the glass up to his mouth without looking at it. But before he took a sip, he inhaled through his nose, and then frowned. He looked down at the drink then, and when he saw it wasn't alcohol, his face scrunched up in disgust.

"Really?" he said.

"I need you to stay focused," Xander said. Nicks had many fine qualities, but knowing when to say no when wasn't one of them. They'd walked into a viper's nest, and they all needed to remain stone-cold sober if they didn't want to get bit.

Nicks didn't look happy, but he nodded. He did not, however, take a sip of his cranberry and club soda.

Xander walked away from the bar, but as he went, he saw Nicks stop a woman passing by him.

"Hey, I bought this for you," he said, handing her the drink. She took it, looking surprised and grateful.

"Really?" she said. "Wow. Thank you."

Instead of waiting to see the woman's reaction, Nicks disappeared into the crowd. Xander followed suit, heading off in a different direction. In his ear, he heard Adele's voice.

"Girls, guns, and global domination. Xander Cage is back."

He smiled. "Did I ever leave?"

* * *

Xiang sat alone at a table in the club's upper balcony, watching the partiers below. He was bored. Out. Of. His. Fucking. Mind. And when a pair of beautiful women approached him and tried to say hi, he ignored them, and they moved on, throwing shade at him as they departed. Xiang didn't care. He wasn't the kind of man who enjoyed satisfying fleeting desires, and he hadn't come here to party. He was enduring this cesspit for one reason only: to lay low until he had the opportunity to use Pandora's Box. Until then, all he could do was sit, wait, and try not to go insane.

At least Talon had no difficulty passing the time here. He was down on the dance floor, tearing it up in a performance that was part acrobatics, part martial arts, and all attitude. People had backed away to give him room, and now a small crowd watched him, clapping and cheering as he executed one seemingly impossible move after another

Xiang saw a large man making his way through the crowd. At first glance, there was nothing special about him. He was tall, fit, muscled, and tattooed, and he exuded absolute confidence, as if there wasn't a man—or woman—in the place that he couldn't take on. A bonafide badass, Xiang thought, but then so were a lot of people here. But what set this man apart were subtle qualities that most people would never recognize. But then Xiang wasn't most people. Outwardly, the man appeared to be just another partier trying to get the lay of the land, checking people out, looking for a bed partner or someone to pick a fight with. Maybe both. But he moved with a relaxed precision that told Xiang this was a man whose mind and body were in perfect balance. And while he looked at the people he passed with what appeared to be only mild interest, Xiang could see the intense concentration concealed in his gaze. This was a warrior, and he'd come here looking for something—or someone.

Xiang smiled. *Now* things were getting interesting.

He let out a piercing whistle, and Talon—hearing the signal—looked up. The two men made eye contact, and Xiang nodded in the warrior's direction. Talon, still dancing, glanced in the direction Xiang indicated, saw the man, turned back to give Xiang a nod, and in the blink of an eye he dropped the party-animal act and became a straight-faced professional. His audience let out moans of disappointment and some urged him to start dancing again, but Talon ignored them as if they no longer existed. He pushed past them and started moving toward the warrior.

Xiang watched Talon's progress, but then the warrior stopped walking and looked up toward Xiang, as if alerted by some instinct that he was being watched. The two men locked eyes, and Xiang could feel an immediate unspoken rivalry between them, a pair of predators recognizing each other for exactly what they were.

Xiang grinned. This just kept getting better and better.

Xander broke eye contact with the Asian man and began making his way through the crowd once more. "I spotted our clown," he said to Nicks and Adele.

"Easier than expected," Nicks replied. *"Drinks all around."*

Xander looked around and spotted Nicks mingling with some *very* hot women not far from the stage. The man knew how to mix business with pleasure, no doubt.

Adele spoke then. *"Tiny dancer on your six, X. I'm ready to have some fun. Douchebag hunting season is my favorite."*

Xander glanced behind him and saw a young Asian man with bleached hair moving in his direction. He recognized him as the man who had been putting on an impressive display on the dance floor only a few minutes ago. He didn't look like a party boy now, though. He looked like a hunter intent on running his prey to ground. He kept his hand pressed tight against his thigh as he walked, and while Xander couldn't see it, he had no doubt the man gripped a knife. Xander pictured Adele sitting in her perch, tracking the man through her rifle's scope, finger on the trigger, ready to put a bullet into the guy's head.

"A little early in the night to kill someone," Xander said.

"*Oh, come on. Let me be Buck Hunter to Mr. Dance Revolution.*"

"*Lemme fix it,*" Nicks said.

The singer and his backup dancers were taking a break, and Nicks hopped up onto the stage and quickly conferred with the man. The singer smiled, nodded, and handed Nicks the mike. A few seconds later, Nicks was standing behind a pair of turntables, hood mask pulled up over his face.

"This a party or a funeral?" he shouted into the mike.

The crowd stopped what they were doing and turned toward the stage, unsure what was happening.

Nicks continued. "Either way… Somebody's get turnt up tonight!"

He put down the mike, reached for the turntables and dropped a massive fucking beat. The crowd cheered in delight and people swarmed the dance floor, gyrating wildly. The man with the bleached hair was cut off from Xander in the bedlam, and Xander took the opportunity to slip away.

"Told you he was fun to have around," he said as he put more distance between himself and his would-be assassin.

Xander made his way to the club's upper level, but when he reached the table where the Asian man had been sitting, he found it empty. He looked around but saw no sign of the man, which was weird. Xander would've seen him come down the stairs, and since he hadn't, that meant the guy was still up here somewhere. This level wasn't very well lit. Lots of shadows for someone to hide in. That was okay, though. Xander didn't mind playing hide and seek.

But before he could start looking, he heard a woman's voice come from close by.

"At first I thought Special Forces, but your ink's all wrong. CIA would send in a drone, bomb us to hell. MI6? Not the kind of subtle they prefer. Who sent you?"

He turned to see a beautiful woman of Indian descent step out of the shadows and into a sliver of moonlight shining through a temple window. She wore a black sports bra, black leather shorts and thigh-high boots. He was impressed. Not many people could get the drop on him like that.

"I haven't been sent anywhere since I got called to the principal's office," Xander said, "and that was in fourth grade."

"The men who come to this island are on the run, hiding from the world. But not you. You're not hiding. You're looking for someone."

He realized then that she was the woman he had seen on the pier, the one who had been watching from a distance before melting into the darkness. She seemed cool as ice, and since she had the advantage over him, he decided to see if he could rattle her a little.

"And who's to say I haven't already found her?" He stepped closer to the woman, forcing her to retreat until her back was literally against a wall. He moved even closer until only a few inches separated them.

If she was intimidated, she sure as hell didn't show it. "Was that meant to scare me?"

Xander smiled. "A little tremble would be nice."

He heard Adele's voice in his ear.

"Really, Cage? She bats her Bambi eyes and suddenly you go jelly on me? Some things never change."

The woman surprised Xander then. She pushed close to him and started running her hands across his body, as if she was trying to turn the tables and intimidate him. Xander decided right then and there he liked this woman. He hoped he wouldn't have to kill her.

"Whatever it is you're here for," she said, "you're gonna come up short."

"I know a Swedish female bobsled team that would beg to differ. But since you think you already know me..."

"Considering that you're one tremble from limping out of here, I'd say I'm pretty close."

Xander felt pressure against his crotch. He looked down and saw that while the woman had been distracting him, she had pressed a gun against his balls.

He looked into the woman's eyes once more. "I'd say

you're a couple inches off."

The woman stiffened as she realized that while she'd pulled a gun on him, he'd pulled a knife on her, and was now pressing the blade to her ribs.

Xander smiled. "Does this mean you're not cooking me breakfast in the morning?"

"I'm gonna be sick," Adele said. *"You know what ruins everything? Boobs."*

Moving lightning-fast, Xander snatched away the woman's gun with his free hand, but moving equally fast, she grabbed his knife, and in the blink of an eye, they both pressed their stolen weapons to the other's throat.

"Bit of a stalemate, sister," Xander said.

"Not if you drop the gun."

"Ladies first."

Neither of them moved an inch.

Xander was finding himself increasingly intrigued by this woman. Not because of her beauty—although he had to admit, that didn't hurt—but because he sensed a fire burning within her, a powerful blaze over which she kept an iron-fisted control. He wondered what would happen if she ever chose to relax her grip and let her fire burn free and wild. If he was close to her when it happened, he thought he might not survive it. But what a way to go.

He decided to give her a bit of the truth and see how she reacted.

"Here's a little secret," he said. "I'm not the bad guy."

She peered deeply into his eyes, and he wondered what she saw there.

"I don't believe in good guys," she said.

Before Xander could respond, he heard a man say, "Serena," and then follow that up with a question in Mandarin. "Who's your friend?"

Xander glanced to the side and saw the Asian man he'd been searching for emerge from the shadows. His expression was calm, almost placid, but his gaze flicked from one weapon to the other, and Xander could practically hear the gears turning in the man's head as he assessed the situation and debated his next move.

"We just met," Serena said.

"But we were getting along famously until you interrupted, Mr. Bad Timing," Xander said.

The man made no move to come closer, but he fixed Xander with an icy stare. "When you leave here, make sure to stick to the path," he said. "There are a lot of unmarked graves on the island."

"Bet the guy who sold you that shirt is in one of 'em," Xander said.

The man's lips tightened in irritation. "How long do you intend to push your luck?"

"As long as it takes to get what I came for," Xander said, looking at Serena.

"Which is what, exactly?" the man said.

Xander and the man in the ugly tropical shirt glared at each other, tension building by the second. And just when Xander thought the man was finally going to lose control and attack him, he removed the gun from Serena's throat, and spoke to the man in perfect Mandarin.

"A damn strong drink," he said.

If the man was surprised that Xander could speak his language, he didn't show it. Instead he motioned for Serena to take her knife away from Xander's throat, and then he smiled.

"That's what I was hoping you would say!"

The man, who introduced himself as Xiang, led Xander and Serena to the table he'd occupied earlier, and the three of them sat. A bottle of Wuliangye—a mellow Chinese liquor that was fifty-three percent alcohol—sat on the table, along with three glasses. Xander poured their drinks and then handed a glass to Serena. "Here you go, precious," he said.

She rolled her eyes at him, but she took the drink. Xander then gave Xiang a glass and took one for himself. He had no idea what was in the pitcher, but whatever it was, it smelled lethal.

"They say alcohol erases all deceit and reveals the hidden truth," Xiang said.

Xander smiled. "I have no hidden truth." He then made a toast in Mandarin. "*Gan Bei!*"

"*Gan Bei!*" Xiang said, then tossed back his drink in a single gulp.

Xander did the same, or at least pretended to. When Xiang's head was tilted back, Xander emptied the contents of his glass over his shoulder. He was certain Serena noticed, but she didn't say anything. Xander put his glass down and gave Serena a wink. She looked at him, her expression unreadable.

She's crazy about me, Xander thought. *She just doesn't know it yet.*

Xiang put his empty glass on the table and then said, "Let's be real and talk about what we *really* want." And then, without further preamble, he reached into his pants pocket, removed an object, and put it on the table, just out of Xander's reach.

It was Pandora's Box.

Tennyson sat on the prow of the bowrider, earbuds in, music blaring while reading redacted documents on his phone. Whenever he encountered a particularly juicy bit of information, he made a note of it on his hand with a black marker.

He was so wrapped up in his reading—who knew that cereal companies were secretly conducting research into parallel dimensions?—that he didn't notice three lights appear on the horizon, heading toward the island.

Helicopters, coming in fast.

6

Xander stared at Pandora's Box. Such a small thing, but it was capable of causing Godzilla-sized destruction.

"Since we're being real, that's all I'm here for," Xander said. "I see no reason you both can't just walk away nicely."

Serena looked at the device with a disgusted expression. "Some people are good at turning their backs when millions of lives are at stake."

Xander frowned. "What's that supposed to mean?"

"Power like that doesn't belong in *anyone's* hands," Serena said. Although she was responding to Xander's question, she locked eyes with Xiang as she spoke.

Looks like there's some conflict in Xiang's merry band of thieves, Xander thought. Good to know.

Xiang scowled at her. "So that's how you wanna play it?"

"Yes," she said, coolly defiant.

There was a satchel on the seat next to Xiang, and he reached into it now and pulled out a grenade. Xander experienced a rush of adrenaline upon seeing the weapon. Xiang popped the pin and rolled the grenade across the table to Xander. He slammed his hand on top of the device, snatched it up, and depressed the trigger, resetting the detonation.

"What is this, Eastern Europe in the nineties?" Adele said. *"Xander, watch out. Next he's gonna send you a fax."*

"You willing to kill people just so you can keep that little contraption for yourself?" Xander nodded toward Pandora's Box.

"Wrong question to ask," Xiang said. His voice was calm and steady, but there was an intensity in his gaze, and Xander knew the man was enjoying this. He was a game-player, a risk-taker.

Takes one to know one, Xander thought.

"What's the right question?" Xander asked.

Serena reached for the box then, but Xiang was faster. His hand was a blur as he drew a knife and slammed it into the table between Serena's hand and the device, the blade missing the tip of her middle finger by only a fraction of an inch.

"Are you willing to *die* for it?" Xiang said.

Time to take this game to the next level, Xander thought. He rolled the grenade toward Serena, and she snatched it up, her reflexes almost as fast as Xiang's.

"One grenade, three people," she said, then smiled. "I like the odds."

She rolled the grenade back to Xander, and he grabbed it once more. Xiang smiled, reached into his satchel, took out another grenade, popped the pin, and rolled it to Serena. She caught it easily, but she didn't look as confident as she had a moment ago.

"Two grenades, three people," Xander said. "I love those odds."

He shot Serena a quick glance, she nodded, and the two of them rolled their grenades toward Xiang. The man caught them without taking his eyes off Xander and Serena. He was smiling now, as if he was enjoying himself immensely. Xander knew just how he felt.

"Give the word, Xander, and I'll put both these assholes out to pasture," Adele said.

Xander reached behind his back and waved her off. The message: *Do NOT shoot!*

Xiang, still holding onto the two grenades, leaned slightly toward Xander.

"You ever bleed so much you open your eyes and all you see is red?" he asked.

"No, but have you ever folded yourself off a triple on a fourstroke and woke up and saw your spleen lying next to you?" Xander looked at Serena. "Bike stalled."

She smiled.

Xiang continued. "When you've fought wars on

every continent, you expect death."

"Naturally," Xander said.

"Our bodies are such fragile things," Xiang said. "Death can sometimes sneak up on you."

Without warning, Xiang rolled the grenades at Xander and Serena with far more force than before, and the two of them barely caught the grenades before they went bouncing off the table. While they were distracted, Xiang drew two more objects from his bag: a third grenade and a 9mm. He placed both objects on the table in front of him.

"Bullet through my throat, drowning in my own blood, and all I can hear myself think is, *Today's the day, today's the day I die*."

Xander thought he understood. It was at moments like those, when death was so close you could feel its cold breath on your skin, that you felt most truly alive.

"Okay, I'm touched," Xander said, "I really am." He called out to a nearby waitress, "Can you bring me my coat from behind the bar, please?"

"I'm not finished," Xiang said. "Then a man comes along, stops the bleeding, and says there are more important things for me to do than die."

Serena pursed her lips in irritation. "Could have saved us all a lot of trouble."

Xiang rolled the third grenade to Serena, who rolled hers to Xander, who in turn rolled his to Xiang.

Xiang continued his story. "Later I'm in a hospital

bed, half-conscious, delirious, and the man comes in and tells me a story about this drought in California, about skateboards and swimming pools. And about a man named Xander Cage."

Xander leaned toward Xiang. "I heard the guy was dead."

Serena smiled knowingly. "Is he now?"

The waitress returned with Xander's coat then, but before she could hand it to him, a loud *whoooooosh* filled the air, and Xander felt the floor vibrate beneath his feet as the building shook. *A helicopter just flew overhead,* he thought. *Military, from the sound of it.* An instant later spotlight beams shone through the windows, and the temple doors burst open and armed soldiers flooded into the club.

The grenade pins had landed on the floor when Xiang popped them. He reached down and grabbed one, reinserted it into the grenade he held, and left the device lying on the floor. He straightened, grabbed Pandora's Box, and shoved it in his satchel, snatched up the bag. He gave Serena a last look before rising from the table and heading off to disappear into the crowd and shadows. But before he vanished, he looked back and gave Xander a "fuck-you" wink.

Serena followed Xiang's lead. She too grabbed a pin, reinserted it into her grenade, placed it on the table, and grabbed the 9mm that Xiang had left behind. She turned to Xander, her expression unreadable, then she slipped away. Unlike Xiang, she didn't look back to give Xander a parting glance.

Xander heard Nicks and Adele speaking in his ear.

"Shit's about to go down," Nicks said.

"Ready to have some fun?" Adele added.

The server who'd been bringing Xander his coat had dropped it on the ground when she fled. He got up from the table, retrieved his coat and headed downstairs, keeping a close eye on the action as he went.

A soldier jumped onto the stage, pointed an assault rifle in Nicks's face, and shouted in a thick Russian accent.

"Turn off music! *Turn it off!*"

Nicks did as the man commanded then put his hands up.

The soldier then turned around and shouted even louder.

"Everybody, hands up! On the floor! First person move, first person die!"

Xander recognized the soldier from a briefing Gibbons had given him years ago. This was Red Erik, Russia's baddest of badasses. While Erik was giving orders from the stage, his men were busy rounding up the partiers and holding them at gunpoint. Xander had reached the ground floor by this point, and he found himself trapped with the prisoners. He saw Serena nearby. He looked around for Xiang, but saw no sign of him. He wasn't surprised. Xiang struck him as one slippery bastard. He wondered if the story the man had told about being approached by Gibbons in the hospital was true, and if so, just what it meant. But he didn't have time to worry about it. He had more pressing problems right now, and they all had Russian accents.

Xander, pulls on his coats, put his hands in his coat pockets and took a step to the side. "I moved," he said.

From the stage, Red Erik looked at him, confused. Xander took a step back to the position where he'd started.

"Oops. I moved again. Why am I still alive?" He looked around at his fellow prisoners. "I mean, *come on*. Is anyone buying this? Russians dropping from the sky? Could you get any more obvious?"

Red Erik had had enough. "Shut up, funny guy."

"OK, alright, OK. Let's do this." Xander said.

As if his words were a cue, the partiers all drew guns—even the women who were barely dressed and didn't seem to have any place on their bodies to conceal weapons. They pointed their guns at the Russians, who suddenly didn't look as sure of themselves as they had a moment ago. The tension in the club increased exponentially as the possibility of violence was quickly becoming a certainty. And once the bullets started flying, everyone in the place—pirate or soldier—would end up as shredded meat lying on the blood-soaked temple floor.

Despite the seriousness of the situation, Red Erik seemed more irritated than worried. "What is this, a bloody circus?"

"I know what you want," Xander said. "I got Pandora's Box right here." He jiggled a hand in his coat pocket to illustrate his point. "You're wrong about something though. You take this from me, you die *first*." Xander nodded to one of the soldiers guarding the crowd. "Lieutenant Leningrad over there goes second. Then the two blond Ivans by the door, Moscow Mule at the bar, and the Igor at the bottom of the stairs after that. Don't get me wrong. I *love* Russia. I hung out with the slednecks in the Red Square. I've gone free diving in the frozen lakes off Siberia. In fact, I spent the best six months of my life on an island called Bora Bora with a beautiful Russian woman named Yelena. But none of that really matters, because like I said, if you take this from me: You. Die. First."

Red Erik sneered. "I take it from you, dead or alive. And if you hold it too tight, I cut your arm off."

Xander caught Serena's eye. He didn't believe in telepathy, but he did believe that like-minded people could communicate in ways beyond mere speech, and if Serena was as sharp as he thought she was, she'd pick up on the vibe he was sending her. After a second, she gave him an almost imperceptible nod, and he turned his attention back to Red Erik.

Xander shrugged. "Okay, suit yourself."

Xander pulled a hand from his coat pocket and tossed an object toward Red Erik. The spy caught the object with a triumphant grin, but when he looked at what he held in his hand, his grin disappeared.

"Grenade?" Red Erik said, surprised. But the Russian recovered quickly, mashing his hand down on the detonator to stop the grenade from exploding. He then gave Xander a "nice try, asshole" smile.

Xander returned the smile as Serena hurled a knife at Red Erik. The blade *thunked* into his wrist, causing him to drop the grenade. The man's eyes went wide as he realized what had happened, and then the grenade exploded, and Red Erik's nickname took on a whole new meaning as chunks of his flesh flew through the air along with copious amounts of his blood.

Just as Xander had promised, the spy had died first.

After that, all hell broke loose as everyone started shooting. Xander spotted two more of Xiang's team—the bleached-haired man who'd tried to kill him earlier and the bearded tough guy who Marke told him had taken out Jonas Borne. The men didn't bother with weapons. Instead they fought with their hands, breaking arms and snapping necks, fury and rage personified, with violent streaks a mile wide.

Xander ran to the soldier he'd dubbed Lieutenant Leningrad, grabbed the man, and slammed him down onto a table, reducing it to splinters and rendering the man unconscious. Xander then saw two soldiers attack Serena. She grabbed the first's gun barrel and pushed it aside before he could shoot her, slammed the heel of her fist into the second one's jaw in a vicious upward strike, and then yanked the gun out of the first soldier's hand and smashed the butt into his skull, dropping him like a rock. She'd taken both men out in two seconds flat.

Damn! The more Xander saw of the woman in action, the more impressed he was by her.

Knowing Serena could defend herself just fine, he turned to head toward the next men he'd promised Red Erik he would take out—the two blond Ivans by the door. But before he could do more than take a step in their direction, the men fell, one after the other. They were followed by Moscow Mule at the bar and the Igor near the stairs.

"That's one more you owe me, Cage!" Adele said. *"You owe me at least 20 more, Xander!"*

Xander grinned and held up three fingers. "Read between the lines!"

He heard the sound of a motorcycle engine racing then, and he looked up in time to see Xiang—the satchel containing Pandora's Box slung over his shoulder—come racing down the stairs on a bike. The man drove straight through the pirates, partiers, and soldiers shooting and brawling, his two men clearing a path for him.

Xander saw Nicks on stage, using the wire from a pair of headphones to choke a Russian soldier. He heard Nicks's voice in his ear and the Russian collapsed to the stage.

"Tennyson! Some backup would be nice!"

"X said stay on the boat!" Tennyson replied.

"That was before the goddamn Russian army touched down, man!"

Another soldier got in Nicks's face with a gun then, and Nicks grabbed the DJ's laptop from the turntable console and snapped it closed over the soldier's gun muzzle. Nicks jerked the gun back and forth, trying to disarm the man, or at least keep him from shooting.

Xander was torn. He wanted to go to his friend's aid, but Xiang was getting away with Pandora's Box, and he couldn't let the man retain possession of such a deadly weapon. Serena's words came back to him now: *Power like that doesn't belong in anyone's hands.* He hated it, but the choice was clear.

Sorry, Nicks, he thought.

Xander hauled ass toward the stairs. He knew there was no way he could catch Xiang on foot, but the man didn't work alone. He had a team. So if he had one bike stashed on the upper level for a quick getaway, there was an excellent chance he had more. As Xander raced up the stairs, he knew what Marke would tell him to do if she were here. *You have a sniper perched in a tree outside, don't you? So tell her to put a bullet through Xiang's head when the asshole rides out of the temple, and call it a fucking day.* He could do that. He *should* do that. But his gut told him it was the wrong call. Maybe it was because of the story Xiang told about Gibbons saving his life and talking to him in the hospital afterward. It sounded as if Gibbons had given the man his Triple-X recruiting speech, and although Xander had no idea why Xiang wanted a weapon of mass destruction so badly, if Gibbons had seen something good in him, then Xander was inclined to give him the benefit of the doubt—at least a little. Gibbons might have presented himself as a cynical smartass, but he wore that persona like camouflage so that people—especially his enemies—would underestimate him. In reality, he possessed the shrewd, calculating mind of a master strategist, and he was an excellent judge of character. In the intelligence game, understanding people—their hopes, dreams, desires, and fears—was perhaps the most important weapon in a spy's arsenal. So if Gibbons saw something in Xiang, then Xander wanted to honor that if he could. After all, if Gibbons hadn't seen that there was more to Xander than most people saw—hell, more than even *he* had seen himself—then Xander Cage wouldn't be the man he was today. He *owed* Gibbons. And Xander always paid his debts.

Once he gained the upper level, Xander ran toward the back, into the shadows, and there he found a black cloth draped over another bike. He tore the cloth away, shrugged off his coat—telling himself that he'd be back to get it—and climbed onto the vehicle. But as soon as he did so, he realized that this wasn't an ordinary motorcycle. This was a fucking *water bike*! He knew the things existed, but he'd never actually seen one before. They were inspired by snow bikes, and they had a paddle tire in the rear, along with a pair of skis mounted on the sides for buoyancy. The vehicles were designed to be amphibious, capable of operating on land or water.

Xander grinned.

He hit the ignition, revved the engine, and shot toward the stairs. The water bike soared over the stairs, and just for the hell of it, Xander did a 360-degree spin in the air before landing in the midst of battling Russians and pirates. As he raced forward, he used the bike as a weapon to take down any soldiers in his way. He spotted Serena in the crowd, her two teammates still busy brutalizing every soldier they could get their hands on, but he saw no sign of Xiang. No surprise. The man had surely made it out of the temple by now, which meant Xander had some catching up to do. As he headed for the temple's entrance, a soldier started shooting at him, so Xander detoured toward the man and lifted up his front wheel to knock the bastard out of the way. The path to the entrance now clear, Xander gunned the engine and the bike surged forward. He saw Serena making her way toward the entrance, too, most likely intending to go after Xiang and Pandora's Box. But as she ran, another soldier stuck out his arm and clotheslined her. She went down, and the soldier—who was armed with a shotgun—gave a nasty grin as he swung the weapon around, intending to shoot Serena in the head.

Xander turned the bike toward the man and gunned the engine. Serena lay on the floor between him and the soldier, and just as the front wheel of the bike was about to strike her, Xander pulled up on the handle bars and goosed the engine. The bike leaped over Serena and smashed into the Russian's chest, sending him flying.

Xander saw the first rays of dawn shining through the temple windows. Time to get moving. But Serena rose to a sitting position and looked up at him, and he couldn't resist performing a bunny hop with the bike for her, jumping both the front and back wheels off the ground several times.

"Trembling yet?" he said, grinning.

She smiled, and then Xander pointed the bike toward the temple entrance and gave it the gas. As he flew past the stage, Nicks threw the soldier he'd been struggling with into his path. Xander rolled over the man—who let out a pained *oomph!*—and then he was out of the temple and in the morning light.

As the bike juddered down the temple steps, he saw a Russian soldier standing guard at the bottom. The man turned toward Xander and raised his assault rifle, but before he could fire, Adele unfurled from her perch, spinning as the sailcloth unwrapped around her. She shot the soldier in the head as Xander roared past the man.

Adele came to the end of the cloth and landed gracefully on her feet.

"That's another one you owe me!" she shouted as Xander raced away.

Nicks ran out of the temple in time to see Xander head off into the jungle after Xiang. Adele ran after him, determined to watch his back even though there was no way in hell she could hope to catch up to him on foot. Then again, if anyone could do it, it would be her. Nicks had never known anyone with more sheer stubbornness in his—

His thoughts broke off as a soldier carrying a 9mm emerged from the temple. The man looked pissed as hell, and when he saw Nicks, he shouted in Russian. Nicks didn't know the language, but whatever the man said, Nicks knew it couldn't be good. *Time to ball out,* he thought, and started running. Unfortunately, the soldier decided to give chase.

Fuck! Nicks had no idea why the man had a hard-on for him. Maybe one of the soldiers Nicks had taken out had been the guy's friend. Or maybe he was pissed that their raid on the temple hadn't turned out like they'd thought it would, and he was looking for someone to take out his anger on. Whatever the reason, Nicks did *not* want the man to get his hands on him, and so he poured on the speed.

The soldier fired as they ran, and Nicks expected to feel a bullet slam into his back any second, but none did. Nicks didn't care what the reason was. He was just happy not to be dead yet.

Nicks made it to the beach and kept running, but he quickly realized that he'd made a mistake. The sand slowed him down, and it wasn't easy to keep his footing. If he wasn't careful—

Nick tripped and went down face-first.

He rolled onto his back in time to see the soldier jogging up to him. The soldier reloaded his gun and aimed at Nicks's head. As he was about to squeeze the trigger the bowrider came flying up onto the beach and slammed into the Russian, crushing the man beneath its weight.

Shocked, Nicks looked up to see Tennyson leaning down and removing his mouth guard.

"X said stay on the boat," Tennyson explained.

Xander raced through the jungle, snapping branches and kicking up dirt as colorful birds took to the air to get out of his way. He had no trouble following Xiang's trail. To Xander's experienced eye, the man might as well have left a trail of coconuts. But Xander had to do more than follow if he wanted to catch up to Xiang. He banked the bike to the left, deviating from the path the other man had taken. The underbrush was thicker here, the trees larger and closer together. Xiang had wisely avoided this part of the jungle, but Xander couldn't afford to play it safe—and he wouldn't have wanted it any other way. He cut through underbrush and weaved through a maze of trees, at times with so little clearance that his arms scraped their trunks. And then he emerged from the labyrinth of green into a more open area, and there was Xiang, leaning forward on his bike and riding like the proverbial bat out of hell.

Xander fell in line behind Xiang and stayed on his tail as they continued blazing a trail through the jungle. And then suddenly, they crashed out onto the beach, but instead of slowing down, Xiang headed straight for the water. He pushed a button and the bike's water skis ratcheted down into place. Xander did the same thing, and then the two men were on the ocean, zooming across the surface without losing any speed, leaving a trail of white spray behind them as they went.

But things were, of course, about to get worse.

Xiang and Xander rode toward a military patrol boat that was anchored offshore. Russian soldiers stood on the deck, and they turned when they heard the bikes draw near, raised their guns, and began firing.

Xiang hunkered down to make himself the smallest

target possible and increased his speed. Xander did the same, and both men weaved their bikes back and forth to make it harder to draw a bead on them. Xiang angled away from the boat, but Xander saw that the crew was already pulling up their anchor, and there were machine guns mounted fore and aft. Men were running toward the guns, preparing to add their firepower to the mix, and Xander knew that once they got that boat moving, he and Xiang would have a hard time outrunning them.

He turned toward the boat and headed straight for it. There was a flare gun in the bike holster, and Xander drew it, took aim, and fired at the boat's gas tank. The flare launched with a *whumpf* and streaked toward the boat. Xander tossed the gun aside, turned away from the boat, and raced away as the green-burning flare struck the tank and the boat exploded into flame. He felt a blast of hot air against his back, but he ignored it and concentrated on catching up to Xiang.

The man was headed out to sea, and he'd put a good amount of distance between them while Xander had detoured to deal with the Russians. Xander gunned the throttle and picked up speed and bit by bit began closing in on Xiang. The farther they went, the rougher the water became, and choppy waves rolled toward them. Xiang and Xander began jumping over the small waves, as if they were snow skiing and jumping over moguls. They jumped in perfect synchronization—up, over, down, and up again.

Xiang took a quick look back and saw Xander not more than a dozen feet behind him.

"Come on!!" he shouted, then faced forward once more.

Xander was gratified to see that he'd rattled the man. If he kept up the pressure, maybe he could rattle Xiang further, and he would start making mistakes. He goosed the throttle again, drawing even closer to Xiang.

On your six, motherfucker, he thought.

The water calmed then, and Xander was able to close the distance even more, until only a couple feet separated the two men.

Just a little more…

But then Xander looked past Xiang and saw a twenty-foot wave approaching them. Xiang headed straight for it, and Xander realized the man intended to surf the damn thing. Xiang didn't lack balls, that was for sure, but then neither did he. Another wave crested, and the two men entered the tube, Xiang banking up the wall, Xander right behind him. Xiang hurdled easily over the crest of the wave, but now it barreled down on Xander, threatening to crash into him. There was no way Xander was going to get over it, so he slammed the front of his bike down and duck-dived under the water, passing easily through the wave and popping out the other side, closer to Xiang than ever.

Another wave crested, and again both men entered the

tube. Xiang banked up the wall with Xander following. This time Xiang had a different trick up his sleeve, though. He drew his bike's flare gun and shot at Xander's vehicle. The green flare tracked through the tube of the wave, reflecting off the water. The flare lodged in Xander's front tank with a *fwump!* It sparked and burned, and then the tank exploded. Xander leaped forward at the same time, and the force of the explosion sent him flying toward Xiang. Grabbing the back of Xiang's bike, Xander put down his feet and surfed the surface of the water.

"You crazy sonofabitch!" Xiang shouted, half in fury, half in admiration.

Xander pushed himself forward and grabbed for the satchel when suddenly a giant wave washed over them, sending them both under.

Water roared in Xander's ears, and the clashing currents spun him around as if he were a rag doll, but he didn't panic. Death wasn't an enemy; it was a friend. It urged you to keep moving, never stop, never give up until the very last tick of the clock and the buzzer sounded. Until that instant—and only then—the game wasn't over. And as long as the game was still on, Xander intended to play it as hard as he could. Maybe it wasn't a game you could win, but it sure as hell was one you could lose, and he *hated* losing.

Xander opened his eyes. He didn't see Xiang, but he did see the satchel, tumbling in the current, just like him.

He kicked hard through the undertow, and reached for the satchel, hand outstretched, straining to reach it. He hadn't had time to do more than take a fast gulp of air before the wave hit, and now his oxygen was almost used up and his lungs burned. He ignored the sensation and kept swimming toward the satchel, reaching, reaching… He felt lightheaded and blackness nibbled at the edges of his vision, and he knew he couldn't last much longer. Still, he swam, still he reached. Almost there…

Xander walked onto the beach. He pulled off his wet shirt, then removed Pandora's Box from the satchel and tossed the bag aside. He was tired and sore, but then he saw Serena waiting, aiming her gun at him. He froze for a moment, but then stared her down.

He held up Pandora's Box for her to see. "I never come up short," he said.

Serena didn't smile at his joke.

"Like I said, power like that doesn't belong in anyone's hands."

Xander held the device out to her. "If you want it, come take it from me."

Serena fired. Xander didn't flinch as the bullet tore Pandora's Box from his grip and sent it tumbling to the sand. Serena fired at the device two more times, destroying it.

Xander grinned. If he'd been in Serena's place, he

would've done the exact same thing.

"Oh come on," he said, "was that really necessary?"

Serena looked at him, her expression dead serious. "I'm Triple-X, too, and it's what Gibbons would have wanted."

She dropped the Glock in the sand, turned, and walked away.

"I'm doing this for Gibbons!" Xander said. He watched Serena go, emotions mixed. A few seconds later, Adele, Nicks, and Tennyson came running along the beach toward him.

"Nice of you guys to show up," Xander said.

"Do you have any idea what just happened?" Adele said. Her face was ashen, her voice shaky. Something was seriously wrong.

Serena heard Adele's words, and she turned around, curious.

"No," Xander said. "What happened?"

"Another satellite just fell," Adele said. "This one on Moscow."

Xander looked at the shattered remains of Pandora's Box lying on the sand. What the actual fuck was going on here?

7

GLOBEMASTER CARGO BAY

Xander and his team were gathered around a monitor, while Becky stood at a table, working on the remains of Pandora's Box. Nicks sat on the floor, his back propped against one of the table legs, drowsing. Marke was present, as was Serena, who stood close to Xander, but not *too* close.

The monitor displayed an image of Luzhniki Stadium, one of the largest and most beautiful sports arenas in the world. Originally built in 1956, it was an Olympic venue in 1980, and many famous singers and entertainers had performed for millions there. The stadium had since been renovated to make it more modern, and it was one of Moscow's premiere attractions.

As the footage rolled, something flashed out of the sky and slammed into the stadium. The impact was devastating, and within seconds nothing remained of the Luzhniki but fire and rubble. The screen froze on the image of absolute destruction, and a long, somber silence followed until Tennyson finally broke it.

"Guess this means Pandora's Box isn't exactly classified anymore," he said.

"The next video footage was broadcast worldwide after the destruction of the stadium," Marke said. She aimed a remote at the screen, and the ruins of the Luzhniki were replaced by a wall of old televisions. Each TV screen displayed a different program, all from the 50s, 60s, or 70s. Variety programs, news broadcasts, police and medical dramas, Saturday morning cartoons, soap operas, political speeches, talk shows, commercials… The audio was spliced together from the footage to "speak" with a single message.

"I'm old enough to remember how things used to be. I remember walking down the street and not being spied on. I remember talking on the telephone and not wondering who was listening on the other line. I remember a world where we trusted our government, and where our lives were our own. Disable and dismantle all the world's spy programs within the next twenty-four hours or I'll do it for you, one satellite at a time. Save the world with your humility or destroy it with your hubris."

The screen went dark then, and Adele turned to Serena.

"Tell me, was this all part of your mission, too?" she asked, voice tight with anger.

"Of course not," Serena said coolly. "Xiang, Hawk, Talon, and I were a new Triple-X team Gibbons created to fight the enemy within, to watch the watchers. We discovered a high-level intelligence officer who was trying to manipulate satellites, but before we could unmask him—" she glanced at Marke "—Gibbons was killed."

"By somebody on the inside." Xander turned to Marke. "You lied to me. And in a church, no less."

"I needed you to retain a sense of objectivity," Marke said.

"I don't understand," Serena said. "I destroyed Pandora's Box, so how did another satellite fall on Moscow?"

Becky joined the rest of them then, and held up the remains of Pandora's Box.

"If I'm right—and I totally am—this box only ever had the ability to control *one* satellite," she said.

Tennyson frowned. "What does that mean?"

Xander knew. "It means we've been chasing a *prototype*."

"Exactly," Becky said, "and that's not a good thing."

"So what do we do?" Tennyson asked.

Xander yawned. "We take a dirt dive."

Marke frowned. "Dirt dive?"

Xander started for the stairs. There were bunks on the upper level, they sounded damn inviting to him right now. He responded to Marke without turning to face her.

"Right now there's nothing I can do, so I'm going to grab some Z's, and I suggest the rest of you do the same.

We've got a hell of a lot of work ahead of us, and we need our beauty sleep if we're going to save the world."

"Some of us need it more than others," Adele muttered.

Xander was too tired to tell her to go to hell. He started up the stairs, his eyes already starting to droop. He hoped the world's satellites would stay in their orbits while he slept. It would be nice to wake up and not have to look at images of more craters in the ground where buildings— and far more importantly, people—used to be.

Xiang and Hawk watched from the roof of a building close to the Manila Airfield as the Globemaster rose into the sky.

"Serena played us for fools, betrayed us," Hawk said, his voice bitter. "We should have seen it coming."

Xiang understood how Hawk felt, but he also understood Serena's point of view. He didn't share it, of course, but he knew she acted based on what she believed was right, and he could respect that.

"This isn't about Serena," Xiang said. "This is *war*. And we either stop it or watch the world burn tomorrow. Can't lose focus on that, alright?"

"Yeah," Hawk said. He didn't sound completely convinced, though.

Talon came up onto the rooftop then and joined them. The Globemaster had dwindled into the distance, and Xiang knew the craft wouldn't be visible much longer.

Hawk turned to Talon and snapped at him, likely taking out some of his anger at Serena on the man.

"Where you been? Stop off for a rub-and-tug?"

Talon smiled as he replied. "That reminds me, your mom says hi."

"Get over here and stop jerking around," Xiang said. "Tracker on board? Nobody saw you?"

"Nobody *ever* sees me, boss," Talon said.

Excellent, Xiang thought. Now wherever Marke took Xander and the others, they would be able to follow.

"Now what?" Hawk said.

"We finish what we started," Xiang said. "But first, let's get something to eat. But no Chinese food, especially from those restaurants. Too much MSG."

Hawk rolled his eyes. "As if that's what'll kill us."

After a couple hours of sleep, Xander and the others gathered in the Globemaster's Command Center. Xander felt sharp once more and ready to get back to work. Becky sat at a console, controlling the images on a monitor, and everyone watched as she displayed security footage from the New York theft. Donovan—one of the NSA monkeys Xander had dropped over Europe—was there too, shooting Xander dark looks periodically. Everyone watched Xiang crash through the window and tackle Marke. Becky then replayed the clip, running it in slow motion.

Xander frowned as he thought. "How often do these

seven men all sit in the same room together?"

"Almost never," Marke said.

Xander continued. "And if you needed retinal scans, cell-phone data dumps, and bio-metrics of all the super-powers in the world, who would you target?"

"Oh, shit," Marke said.

"Call me crazy," Adele said, "but I personally would hand-select all seven of those spymasters and get them around a big giant table for a meeting. But then that's impossible, right?"

"You gotta give this player—whoever he is—props," Nicks said. "I mean, he scammed the smartest dudes in the world. Real heist movie kinda shit."

"True," Xander said, "but I think the real question is who's got the kind of power to set all this in motion?"

Xander turned to face Marke and gave her a pointed look.

"Oh, you are pissing up the wrong tree, Cage," she said. "*I* came looking for *you*, remember?"

Donovan stepped between Xander and Marke and grabbed hold of Xander's arm. "We gonna have problems, asshole?"

Xander grinned. "Look, everyone! It's Peter Pan! Did you enjoy your flight, Donovan?" Then he grew serious. "No, no problem. I'm just doin' the math."

Donovan scowled. "What math?"

"Air velocity divided by distance," Xander said. He

took hold of Donovan's wrist and pulled his hand away from his arm. "Because if you touch me again, I'm gonna throw you a beatin' and then shove you down the toilet so far that Search and Rescue is gonna have to look for you in China."

Donovan stepped forward a couple inches until their noses were almost touching. "Keep talking, punk."

Xander was ready to kick the man's ass on general principle, but Becky was running the security footage again, and this time he noticed something he hadn't before.

"Hold that thought, G.I. Joe." Xander pushed past Donovan and stepped closer to the monitor. "Run it one more time, Becky."

She did so, and Xander saw it again. "Okay, freeze it there." He turned to Marke. "Okay, you're off the hook, Suit. You didn't do it."

"Why thank you," she said. "So who did?"

"Isn't it obvious?" Xander said.

She crossed her arms and gave him a look that said her patience was wearing thin. "Enlighten me."

"The man who hosted the party," Xander said. He turned to Becky. "Scroll back a little. More... Stop."

The image displayed on the monitor was a freeze-frame shot of Xiang crashing through the conference room window. Xander picked up a black marker from a nearby workstation and circled the CIA director.

"He's the only one of the seven men who didn't flinch when Xiang busted through the window," Xander said.

Everyone leaned in for a closer look. It was a small detail, but now that Xander had pointed it out, it was obvious. Even Donovan looked impressed—a little, anyway. Though it didn't stop Becky freaking out over the damage to her monitor.

Marke immediately took out her phone and placed a call.

"I need the President on the phone ASAP. I want the joint chiefs and the executive directorate. We have a snake in the house."

"Oh, *now* you all start paying attention," Tennyson said, exasperated. "I've been saying the director of the CIA has been trying to destroy the world for *years*!"

Marke finished her call and disconnected.

"We have carte blanche to track this motherfucker down," she said. "Does anybody know how to do that?"

"The same way Xiang and I found the prototype in New York," Serena said. "Pandora's Box needs to keep reconnecting itself because the satellites orbit." Serena stepped to the console Becky had vacated and began typing commands. "All we need to do is track down the main signal."

A map appeared on the monitor, showing the general location of the Director and Pandora's Box.

Adele frowned. "So he's got the whole world to lay low

in and this fruit loop chooses Detroit?"

"It wouldn't be *my* first choice," Becky said, "but then I'm not a sociopath."

Xander's expression darkened as he looked at the map. Serena rose from the console, stepped to his side, and put a hand on his arm. "Is something wrong?" she asked softly.

"Been a long time since I've been in Detroit," he said, and left it at that. But in his mind, he pictured a dead thirteen-year-old boy lying in the street.

"Triple-X," Marke said, "are you ready to take it to the next level?"

Xander smiled grimly. "Am I ready? Hell, I was *born* ready."

DOWNTOWN DETROIT

The city had undergone quite a few changes since Xander had last been here, but Detroit still had its problems. Even if the city still had a lot of work to do, Xander was encouraged by the improvements. He wondered if Gibbons had ever returned to the city to see how much it had changed. He hoped so.

A battered yellow van pulled up to the curb in front of a rundown building next to an electrical substation. Tennyson parked and he, Adele, Becky, and Nicks climbed out and began unloading their gear.

"Do I want to know where you got these wheels?" Nicks asked.

"No, you don't," Tennyson said.

They carried their equipment into the building, which served as an NSA safehouse, and headed for a room in the back. Becky had never been in a place even remotely like this. It smelled like someone with assholes in their armpits had lived here, and she was afraid to breathe too deeply, let alone actually *touch* anything.

Tennyson and Nicks talked as everyone continued walking further into the building.

"When I crashed the boat up on shore and saved your life—" Tennyson began.

"Yeah, whatever, bro," Nicks said.

"—do you think that counts as crash one ninety-nine for me? You know, officially?"

Nicks rolled his eyes. "Officially, you're deranged."

The door to the backroom was locked and refused to budge. Tennyson put the equipment he was carrying down on the floor, made a fist, drew back his arm, and punched the door open. He then stepped aside and gestured for the others to enter.

"Nice job, big guy," Adele said as she walked past him. The others followed, with Tennyson bringing up the rear.

The room smelled marginally better than the rest of the building, Becky thought. There was a chance she'd only catch two or three fatal diseases in here instead of several dozen. The room had some simple furniture in it—a table, chairs, and a couch that had seen better days. Hell, better *decades*. But there were large plastic-covered objects lined against the wall. They put their equipment down and removed the covers to reveal a number of badass, teched-out Triple-X toys. Becky couldn't wait to get her hands on these goodies and start going to town.

Nicks went to the window to open the blinds, but when he pulled on the string, the entire thing came off and crashed to the floor.

"Nicks…" Adele said.

"I can fix it," Nicks said.

Normally, Becky might've laughed at Nicks's expression, but despite her excitement at seeing all this awesome tech, she couldn't escape the feeling that she was making a massive mistake. She stepped to Adele's side and spoke to the woman in a hushed voice.

"I really should not be here. I am *not* a field agent. I mean, I understand you guys need someone on the ground, but *come on*, what do I do if somebody starts shooting at me?"

Adele gave her a measured look before answering.

"Duck," she said.

Adele then turned away to continue assembling her equipment, leaving Becky standing alone.

All right, Xander, she thought. You said the outside is where the fun is. You damn well better be right.

She joined the others, and together they continued setting up shop.

In a downtown Detroit apartment, the Director stood in front of a bank of monitors kludged together from spliced cables and hacked telephone lines. The screens displayed various video images and data feeds, and the Director took in all the information as easily as a sponge absorbed water. He wiped sweat out of his eyes and off his lower face. The room was hotter than motherfucking hell, but it couldn't be helped. He was just going to have to put up with it.

Jonas Borne hauled a propane heater into the room. He set it up next to a dozen others and then turned it on.

When Borne was finished, he joined the Director at the monitors. "Let me guess. Everyone's not exactly jumping at the chance to dismantle their spy programs."

"The world's too stupid to believe that Moscow wasn't a bluff," the Director said. And really, he hadn't expected anything different.

"So what do we do?" Borne asked.

"Lay down our hand."

The Director held Pandora's Box—the *real* one, not the shitty prototype he'd let Cage and his dysfunctional band of misfits chase—and now he activated it. One of the monitors displayed a list of satellites, and using Pandora's Box like a remote, he scrolled through the list until he came to the one he wanted. He then selected a target.

Rome. The Vatican.

The Director wiped sweat from his brow and smiled.

Xander and Serena were on the roof of a building on an industrial pier near the Riverfront.

He and Serena worked to assemble an antenna array; as they did, they heard Becky's voice in their ears.

"Once the array's installed, I'll be able to triangulate Pandora's signal to within a hundred feet anywhere in the city," she said.

As they finished up the job, Serena said, "You know, one thing I never understood. Why fake your death? Why walk away from the world when it needed you the most?"

Xander considered how much he wanted to tell her. He decided on the short version. "Gibbons recruited me because he needed a rebel to protect the people of this world. Turns out I was only protecting the people on top. You can't fight the man if you work for him."

They made a few final adjustments, then Becky performed some tests, pronounced everything "fine as wine," and Xander and Serena packed up their tools and started down the stairs.

As they descended, Xander asked, "What about you?"

"Me?" Serena said.

"How did you get into all this? The Triple-X program, I mean."

"Tagged a skyscraper. Got a year in jail for it."

"A year? Seems excessive."

"Tag was thirty stories tall. Two million hits on YouTube. I served only half my sentence."

Xander grinned. He was going to have to check out that video. "Let me guess. Gibbons to the rescue."

"Yep. He said a lion like me didn't belong in any kind of cage." She stopped on a landing and pulled up her sleeve to reveal a lion tattoo.

"Yeah, that's why I got this after I left the NSA." Xander pulled up his sleeve to reveal a similar tattoo, and Serena smiled. He noticed another on her left wrist: a Ferris wheel.

"Where did you get that one?" he asked.

"London, 2009, climbed the Millennium Wheel..." She paused, then added, "Naked."

"Naked?" He smiled. "Where was I?"

He lifted his shirt to reveal a tattoo around his nipple: a circle of fire.

"High school," he said.

Serena laughed. "Nooo!"

"We all have things we're embarrassed about," Xander said, lowering his shirt. "What about that beautiful one above your belly?" It was a stylized image of a bull's face.

"Running with the bulls, 2011. Last woman standing. Last man standing, actually."

"Impressive. Try doing that with elephants." Xander rolled up his right sleeve to reveal the massive elephant tattoo on his arm. Xander pointed to one on her left hip and waist, a graceful image of a bird. "What about that sexy one right there?"

"Phoenix out of the ashes," she said. "Fourteen hours in a chair in Mexico. Drank my body weight in tequila to get through it. It's the most important one, actually. It was when I decided to change the world rather than rage against it. I saw the wings on your back at the beach."

"Some ink you don't explain," he said. Then, more to change the subject than anything else, he reached out and brushed her hair away from her neck. "What about this beautiful one on your neck?"

It was a sphere that radiated beams of light.

"New York, 2014," she said. "Dick Clark's New Year's Rockin' Eve. I dropped the ball twenty minutes early."

"They say the ribs are the most painful." Xander lifted his shirt once more to reveal his ribcage. "I got this one straight and sober. It's a tigress. I got it right after I watched this crazy girl drop the ball ten minutes before I was about to. New York City, 2013. I was standing in the square."

Her eyes widened in surprise and she smiled in delight. "You saw me across the square?"

"Nah, I saw you across the city."

Without realizing it, they had pushed very close to one another. Serena leaned toward him, and he leaned toward her. But just as their lips touched, Becky shouted in their ears, spoiling the moment.

"We found him! We've got Pandora's Box!"

They broke apart, but as they looked into each other's eyes, Xander knew that whatever was happening between them wasn't over. It fact, it was only beginning.

Xiang, Talon, and Hawk sat inside a van, parked only a block away from the NSA safehouse. Xiang sat behind the wheel, cigarette in hand, window open to allow the smoke to drift out. Hawk sat in the passenger seat, staring out the window and tapping his fingers on the dash, jonesing for some action. And Talon sat in the back, laptop open next to him, the screen mirroring Becky's workstation display. They'd followed Xander's friends to the safehouse, and Talon had managed to slip in through another entrance, find the equipment room, get inside, plant the signal-cloning device, relock the door, and get out before the NSA team reached the room.

Nobody ever sees me, boss.

Xiang couldn't dispute that.

"This is it!" Talon said. He slid a finger across the screen, increasing the volume. Becky's voice came through the laptop's speaker.

"We found him! We've got Pandora's Box!"

Xiang smiled, took a quick drag on his cigarette, and then tossed it out the window. "Not if we find him first."

Talon gave him the Director's location: a penthouse in a downtown apartment building. They could be there within minutes. Feeling the anticipation of a hunter closing in on his prey, Xiang started the van, put it in gear, gunned the engine, and peeled away from the curb.

In their own van, Xander's team raced down the street. Tennyson drove and Nicks rode shotgun, but from the queasy expression on Nicks's face, it looked as if he now regretted his choice of seat.

Serena and Adele sat in the back, and while they maintained their composure more effectively than Nicks, it was clear from the way they gripped the seat that they weren't any more relaxed than he was.

Xander sat in the middle seat, arms spread out, smiling. *At least someone is enjoying the ride,* Tennyson thought.

He drove like a maniac, even by his standards, swerving though traffic, scraping cars and clipping side mirrors. Blaring horns, squealing tires, and shouted obscenities followed in his wake, the sounds like soothing music to him. He laughed with delight and turned to look at Nicks. But the man was looking straight ahead, an expression of horror on his face.

"Red light! Red light! Red light!" Nicks shouted.

Tennyson zoomed through the intersection squeezing between two trucks with only inches to spare.

"You know traffic signals were invented by Big Oil to waste fuel and drive up profits, right?" Tennyson said.

"If I say yes, will you please *slow down*?" Nicks pleaded.

× × ×

* * *

In the back seat, Serena did her best to ignore Tennyson's suicidal driving, but it wasn't easy. Ever since they'd gotten in the van, Adele had avoided eye contact with her, and she could sense the woman's hostility toward her. Serena wasn't the type of person to avoid a confrontation, and if they were going to function as teammates, they needed to clear the air.

"Is this the part where you act the basic bitch and tell me you've got your eye on me and that you don't trust me?" Serena asked.

Adele finally turned to look at her. "Yes, this is that moment." She sighed. "Listen, you have to understand, for five years I've been carrying around a phone. And there's only one person in the world who had the number." She nodded toward Xander. "*That* butthead. And he called because he needed me, so I'm here. And now you're here."

Adele paused and Serena understood what the woman was leaving unsaid—and what it was costing her *not* to say it. Adele and Xander had been close once. *Very* close. And although that time was over, it was clear she would do anything for him. Serena appreciated that kind of loyalty. It was a rare thing, but Xander engendered it in the people whose lives he touched.

Adele continued. "So look, it's nothing personal. I think it's just as likely you'll stab him in the back as save his life. But hey, I don't trust kittens, so why don't you prove me wrong?"

Adele drew her Glock and slapped it into Serena's hand.

Serena understood that the woman had done more than simply give her a weapon. She smiled. "Thanks."

"Stopstopstop!" Nicks yelled.

They had pulled onto an expressway overpass, and ahead of them, traffic was stopped dead. Tennyson slammed on the brakes, and the van started skidding. Serena thought the vehicle might flip over, but Tennyson managed to get the van back under control, and he was able to stop before slamming into the car ahead of them.

Xander peered out the window at the gridlock.

"All right, we're gonna have to hoof it," he said.

Xander and the team got out of the van. They checked their gear and bumped fists, psyching each other up in preparation for what was to come. Xander took a phone from his pocket and handed it to Serena.

"If you run into trouble, dial nine," he said.

She nodded and took the phone. "Promise me you'll destroy it."

Xander didn't answer. Instead, he looked toward an apartment building in the distance. That was it: their target. The Director was in that building, holed up in the penthouse. He had the device with him, and he could use it at any moment. He turned to Adele. She'd slipped on her rifle backpack and was ready to rumble.

"Find higher ground," he said.

"I'm one step ahead of you," she said, and after exchanging a parting glance with Serena, she started running.

Xander turned to Tennyson. "Stay with the boat."

Before he could say anything to Nicks, he caught sight of Xiang two lanes over, unloading a van with Hawk and Talon. Xiang looked over, as if he sensed Xander's presence, and the two men locked eyes.

"You crash my party, I'm gonna crash yours," Xiang shouted. To Hawk and Talon, he said, "Kick their asses!"

"This ain't a party," Nicks said. "This is a *race*. Get him, X!"

Xiang jumped onto the back of a car and then onto the guardrail. Without hesitation, he leaped off the rail and dropped out of sight.

Xander started to run after Xiang, only to find his way blocked by Hawk. Xander didn't slow down. Before the man could make a move, Xander grabbed him by the shoulders, spun him around, pinned his arms against his back, and frogmarched him toward the guardrail.

"What the hell do you think you're doing?" Hawk demanded.

"Building a ramp!" Xander said.

He shoved Hawk onto the guardrail, stepped on his

back, then onto his shoulders, and then used him as a springboard. He leaped into space and plummeted toward the expressway below.

8

Xander landed on a ten-ton truck driving under the expressway, immediately lost his footing, and tumbled down the too-short cargo box before dropping off the back. He desperately grabbed for the rear edge of the roof and snagged hold of it, hanging on with the grip of an experienced free-climber. His body banged against the truck's rear cargo door, but he gritted his teeth against the pain and held on, refusing to let go.

Just another day at the office, he thought.

"Go, go, go!" Serena shouted, urging her new teammates to scatter. Adele was already gone, having run past the lines of stopped cars, across the overpass, and into the neighborhood on the other side, where she turned down an alley. Tennyson and Nicks ran back to the van, and Serena turned to head in the direction they'd come from. She remembered the van zooming past a car-parts junkyard before getting onto the overpass, and she headed in that direction now. Unfortunately, Talon followed after her in hot pursuit, and it was her turn to run a race.

Let's see just how fast you are, my friend, she thought, and poured on the speed.

As Tennyson once more got behind the wheel of the van, he saw Hawk open the door of another van—a beat-up yellow delivery truck. Hawk pulled out the driver, threw him to the ground, and got in. Hawk threw the vehicle into reverse and began backing up.

Nicks and Tennyson jumped back in their van, and jammed it into reverse. The van smashed into a car that had pulled up behind them, but Tennyson continued clumsily backing up, sideswiping a couple more vehicles as he went.

Hawk had backed up far enough now that he had room to turn around. He did so, and then drove off, quickly picking up speed. Tennyson managed to get their van turned around as well, and then he and Nicks hauled ass after Hawk. The chase was on!

Serena reached Bennett's Auto Salvage and raced inside, Talon hot on her heels. They moved swiftly through the junkyard, Serena pulling open car doors as she passed to create a maze of metal she hoped would slow Talon down.

It did—if only a little—and she managed to put some distance between them. But Talon grew tired of navigating Serena's makeshift labyrinth, and he hopped up onto the roof of a car to get a better view. Serena made sure that he saw her, then she ducked out of sight, and slipped into a waiting car.

She heard Talon leap from vehicle to vehicle as he searched for her, and when she judged he was close, she popped up through the car's open sunroof and trained her Glock on him.

She smiled. "Looking for someone?"

Talon made a disgusted face and raised his hands in surrender.

Thanks for the gun, Adele, she thought.

Xander managed to pull himself up just far enough to see over the truck, and he spotted Xiang kneeling on top of a tractor trailer only a little further ahead in traffic. A bus was in the process of passing the truck, and Xander saw his chance. He pulled himself onto the truck's roof, jumped to his feet, and started sprinting. In one continuous run, he reached the front of the truck's cargo box, leaped onto the bus seconds before it passed, kept going as the bus pulled up even with Xiang, and then he leaped onto the tractor trailer and charged straight toward the man. Xiang turned at the last second and realized too late that Xander had caught up with him. Xander slammed into him and the two men pitched off the trailer and slammed onto the roof of an SUV below.

But then the driver of the SUV reacted to having a pair of heavy objects land on his roof. He hit the brakes, and Xander and Xiang flew off the roof and hit the street. The SUV slid out of control and swerved into oncoming traffic, just missing the two men as they tumbled to a stop. But the car behind them raced toward them. Xander instinctively put up his hand to shield himself as the car's driver braked to a stop only inches from his face. Xander rolled away from the vehicle straight into a kick from Xiang, who was lying on his side. With Xander momentarily stunned, Xiang leaped to his feet and started running through traffic.

Xander gave chase as Xiang cut straight into oncoming traffic. Drivers swerved desperately to avoid hitting him, but the drivers' erratic movements made it difficult for Xander to avoid their vehicles, and he knew that Xiang had done this on purpose in an attempt to slow him down.

Smart, he thought. *Not to mention ruthless as hell.*

Another car lost control and slid right at Xander, but he hurdled over the car like he was pulling the most intense kick flip of his life, and then he followed that maneuver by 360ing over a car, tracking an invisible skate-line that only he could see. Xander continued moving over and around vehicles in the same manner, giving a gold-medal X-Games performance as he caught up to Xiang.

As Xander passed Xiang, he shouldered him into the path of an oncoming pickup truck, which the man narrowly avoided by executing a brilliant aerial flip. Xander was ahead for the moment, but then he was clipped by a car's mirror, which—while doing no real damage—slowed him down, helping Xiang close the distance with him. Xiang swept Xander's right leg out from under him, and Xander went down. Xiang sprinted past, but Xander expertly rolled and came back up on his feet. He picked up speed, and as he drew close to Xiang, he grabbed hold of the man's collar from behind and jerked the man back into second place.

A few strides later, Xiang grabbed Xander's arm and tried to pull it backward, but Xander, strong as a fucking bull, kept his arms pumping and pulled Xiang forward. Xiang spun around in front of Xander, released his grip on Xander's arm, and put his back to him, forcing him off stride. Xander grabbed hold of Xiang and started to pull him backward once more, when Xiang was clipped by a passing vehicle. The impact sent Xiang airborne, and Xander was pulled along with him. The two men helicoptered through the air and landed hard in the middle of the street.

They lay together, stunned, as cars raced past all around them. Another car came barreling straight toward them, and they managed to roll in opposite directions as the vehicle zoomed through the space they'd occupied only a split second before. As they rolled, two more vehicles narrowly missed taking their heads off, and then both men jumped to their feet and rushed toward each other. Xiang attacked Xander with a kick combination that drove him back into traffic. But as Xiang launched into a finishing back kick, Xander stepped forward and caught Xiang's leg and spun him off balance into the next lane. Xiang instantly regained his balance, but before he could do anything, a van hit him and punched him down the street. The driver, undoubtedly horrified, slammed on her brakes and came screeching to a halt.

Xander chuckled. "Gotcha," he said, but his gloating was short-lived. A swerving truck struck him, sending him flying down the street to land right beside Xiang. The two men looked up at the same time and locked eyes.

"Think I found my new favorite sport!" Xander said.

"Gonna have to fight me for the gold!" Xiang replied.

They smiled at each other then, and Xander thought that in other circumstances they might actually be friends.

But there was no time for sentiment. Xiang kicked out at Xander, but this time he was ready. He deflected the blow and gave Xiang a punch that sent him tumbling. Xander rose to his feet and started running once more, but Xiang quickly recovered and gave chase, and he soon overtook Xander. An approaching car slid to a stop to avoid hitting the two of them, but a second car plowed into it, and a third car swerved, trying to avoid a collision, but it couldn't avoid hitting the second car. The impact flipped the third car into the air—right toward Xander and Xiang. Xander moved without thinking. He grabbed Xiang and dove to the ground as the car flipped over them with inches to spare. When it struck the street, its gas tank exploded, and a wave of heat rolled over the two men, and chunks of metal and engine parts rained down around them.

Xander rose to his feet, and held out a hand to Xiang. After a moment's reluctance, Xiang allowed Xander to help him up.

"Thanks," Xiang said. He sounded sincere, and Xander had no reason to doubt him. He'd saved the man's life, and they both knew it.

"Don't mention it," Xander said.

He elbowed Xiang in the face and started running. Xiang shook off the attack and took off after Xander. The apartment building where the Director was preparing to use Pandora's Box was now only a block away.

Adele raced up the stairs of a dusty rotted tenement across the street from the Director's building. She found a room she thought was suitable, smashed out the window and then quickly set up her sniper rifle. When she was ready, she took aim at the penthouse across the street.

"Do you have eyes on the target?" Becky said in her ear.

Adele scoped the building, but there was only one

penthouse window visible, and she knew the Director wasn't stupid enough to stand in front of it. She switched her scope to thermal imaging and saw that the entire top floor was a red bloom of light.

"Dammit! Bastard's got the heat turned up. I can't see *shit* inside."

"Kinda genius, actually. Almost have to respect it," Becky said.

"Give a man enough time, he'll always make a mistake," Adele replied. "So now we wait."

Xiang jumped over a wall and into an alley, Xander on his heels. Xiang rolled over the hood of a parked pickup truck and launched into a 360-degree flip as Xander rolled off the truck hood right after. Xiang executed a spin kick, knocking a box on top of a dumpster, sending debris flying at Xander.

Xiang then ran toward a fire escape, Xander close behind. Xander caught up to Xiang, grabbed hold of him, and flipped him over. Xiang kicked out, but Xander dodged the strike and leaped up to the fire escape. He began running up the metal stairs, but Xiang jumped onto the fire escape and gave pursuit. The two men raced up three stories until Xander reached a door. He kicked it open and entered the building, Xiang right behind.

* * *

Tennyson and Nicks managed to stay on Hawk's bumper, but no matter how hard Tennyson pushed the van's engine, they couldn't quite catch up. In the distance, they saw the apartment building where the Director had set up his operation.

"Don't let him reach the penthouse!" Nicks said.

Tennyson could think of only one option, and he knew Nicks wasn't going to like it. "I have a plan. *Hold on.*" Tennyson fit his mouth guard into place.

Nicks's eyes went wide with fear. "*Hold on* ain't no goddamn plan! Shit!"

Nicks braced himself as Tennyson veered onto the sidewalk, gunned the engine to draw even with Hawk's vehicle, and then swerved their van into his. The two vans collided, flipped, and tumbled, Tennyson laughing the whole time. Seconds later, the vehicles came to a halt, Hawk's on its side, Tennyson and Nicks's van upside down.

Nicks crawled from the wreck shaken and bloody, but Tennyson figured he'd be all right. He glanced over at the van and saw Hawk lying behind the wheel, eyes closed. Unconscious. Tennyson hung upside down in the van, held in place by his seatbelt. He took his phone from his pocket, grinned, and snapped a selfie.

"That's two hundred!" he said.

Xander and Xiang raced up the fire escape stairs, both men aiming for the top floor and getting closer with every step. But when they were within a couple floors of the penthouse, gunfire suddenly rained down on them. Xander looked up and saw Jonas Borne firing at them from the penthouse's fire escape.

Borne smirked. "Fish in a barrel."

Xander ducked the gunfire, and Xiang jumped onto the railing on his level and leaped up one level *above* Xander, tapping his foot against the wall as he landed. Both men then looked up at Borne.

"Forty-five USP," Xander said.

"Twelve-round mag," Xiang added.

"Five left."

Xiang stuck his foot on the railing and gunshots landed around it. Xiang quickly withdrew his foot.

"Three," Xiang said.

Xander nodded, and without another word being exchanged between them, a plan was formed.

Xander continued up the fire escape, passed Xiang, and continued upward toward Borne. Meanwhile, Xiang distracted Borne by sticking his head out and giving the superspy a target to shoot at. Xander reached the balcony as Borne was taking aim, a sadistic smile on his face. Before the man could shoot, Xander grabbed his wrist and threw him over the railing. Borne fell and landed on the level just above Xiang. Xiang raced up to Borne, who was just rising to his feet, an expression of mingled fury and desperation on his face. He still had hold of his gun, and he raised it, ready to fire. But before he could, Xiang grabbed hold of him and flipped him over the railing, sending him down to the bottom of the stairwell. Borne landed with a horrible thud and the sickening sound of his neck snapping.

Xander looked down over the railing at Borne's dead body. "Empty," he said.

Xiang nodded.

Then Xander turned and entered the penthouse apartment, as Xiang hurried to catch up.

Once inside, Xander saw no one. He saw a bank of cobbled-together set of monitors sitting on a table, and he recognized them as the ones the Director had used to deliver his ultimatum to the world. The screens were still active, displaying various images and scrolling lines of data. But what caught Xander's attention was a small device sitting on the desk in front of the monitors: Pandora's Box.

A number of propane heaters were lined up against a wall. They were all on full blast, and they'd made the apartment feel like the Mojave at high noon. Xander had only been in here for a few seconds, and he could already feel beads of sweat forming on his body.

Xiang entered the room then, but instead of racing to grab Pandora's Box, he took a seat in a chair, relaxed, and lit a smoke.

"Gibbons always thought you'd be back," Xiang said, "and be the hero we needed."

Xander answered without turning around. "I never promised him I'd be a hero."

"You take that box to the NSA, we're right back where we started," Xiang said.

Xander's hands balled into fists, but he pushed all frustrations aside. He'd found the Box, and he'd give it to Marke and let *her* worry about the damn thing. Then maybe the world would leave him in peace.

"Not my problem," he said.

Xiang took a drag on his cigarette, exhaled, and then gave a slow clap of sarcastic applause. "Looks like the Xander Cage Gibbons spoke of really *did* die all those years ago, huh? We needed Triple-X, and you left us behind. You left *Gibbons* behind."

Xander wondered what Gibbons would say if the man were still alive and here right now. Gibbons had been the only one to see the potential within him, something not even Xander saw. Xander hadn't wanted to believe it, had fought against accepting it, but Gibbons's faith in him had never wavered. Not once. And because of that faith, Xander had finally come to realize that maybe— just maybe—Gibbons had been right about him all along.

Well, shit, Xander thought. *Maybe I am the hero after all.*

Just then the Director stepped out from the hallway where he'd been hiding, clothes soaked with sweat, hair plastered to his head. He gripped a 9mm, and he pointed it at Xander.

"Wow, that's really touching," the man said. "The Gibbons Sisters."

Keeping his weapon trained on Xander, the Director stepped to the table and grabbed Pandora's Box.

"I'm walking out of here," he said.

"Not if you keep pointing that gun at me," Xander said.

The Director smiled. "I wonder if you'd be so charming lying in a pool of your own blood."

"I'd like to think so."

"Xiang. Xander didn't kill Gibbons, you dumb bastard. I did. You wanna know why? Because he was a self-righteous prick who thought he could police the world all by himself. He sent his team after me." The Director paused, and then in a calmer voice asked, "Want to know a secret?"

"You failed your psych evaluation?" Xander said.

The Director ignored the jab. "I'm *never* going to stop dropping satellites. You know why? Because the world is a shithole, and we let it get this way. You, me, him, Gibbons … all of us."

"I'm not a fan of this world," Xander said, "but the answer isn't blowing up thousands of people."

"Thousands of people?" The Director laughed. "This is a war for our *survival*. Millions of people die in war."

"I'm not like you," Xander said. "I'm an American. You're from Washington."

The Director had advanced on Xander as they talked,

pushing him back toward the open balcony door. A breeze filtered in through the opening, and the air was slightly cooler here.

Xander heard Adele's voice in his ear then.

"X, I've lost you all in the heat. Thermal's no good. I can't believe I'm saying this, but there's no shot."

Xander took a step closer to the open balcony door, raised his right hand, and gave the Director a three-fingered salute. "Read between the lines," he said to the man, but the message was really for Adele.

Out of the corner of his eye, Xander saw Xiang silently rise from the chair and begin slowly making his way outside the heat circle generated by the propane heaters.

Xander kept his hand up as he spoke. "I had an aunt in the restaurant business, and she had a saying: You can't put out a fire with fire."

"What are you talking about?" the Director said, incredulous. "We fought fire with fire in World War II, and we won!" The man practically screamed these last few words.

"Take it easy," Xander said.

But the Director continued ranting. "I mean, hell, if you're not trying to reboot the world, what's the point of getting out of bed in the morning? Am I right?"

"Okay, something's been bugging me," Xander said. "You got something in your teeth. Right there."

He bent his middle finger so the tip pointed to the

Director, making a perfect gunsight for Adele.

The Director looked confused. "What?"

Adele fired. The bullet flew through the open balcony door, passed through the narrow space between Xander's index and ring fingers, and struck the Director in the face. The man's head snapped back in a spray of blood, and he fell to the floor, dead.

Xander gazed down at the man's corpse. "That was for talking shit about Gibbons, you dumb bastard."

"Next time I'll do it blindfolded." Xander could hear the grin in Adele's voice. It was a one-in-a-million shot, and she knew it.

Xiang stepped to Xander's side, and the two men looked down at Pandora's Box, which still rested in the Director's hand. Neither made a move for the device, and Xander knew it was because at this point, both were willing to let the other have it.

The apartment door burst open then, and Donovan led a team of armed NSA operatives into the room, followed closely by Marke.

Donovan pointed his assault rifle at Xiang. "Get on your knees!" he ordered.

Xiang gave Xander a look that said, *Are you really surprised by this?* Then he put his hands on his head and knelt as operatives surrounded him and trained their weapons on him.

Marke walked toward the Director's body. She glanced

at the red ruin that had been the man's face without reaction. Then she knelt, took Pandora's Box from his hand, and straightened.

"Perfect timing," Xander said. "It's Johnny Come Lately and the Bozo Patrol."

"Watch out, Cage," Marke said. "Keep this up and people might mistake you for one of the good guys." She looked at Donovan. "I want this place scrubbed in twenty minutes, stem to stern."

Donovan nodded, took out a phone, and placed a call.

"You got what you wanted, Suit," Xander said. "We both know Xiang's not the bad guy here. Let him go."

"And who do we blame for Moscow?" she countered. "Better a living terrorist than a dead company man. See what I'm saying?" She turned to address Donovan and his team. "Back on the plane. I want wheels up in twenty."

She walked out of the apartment, leaving Xander to wonder if he'd done the right thing.

Donovan finished his call and put his phone away. "All right, boys. Let's go!"

The team headed for the door, roughly pulling Xiang along with them. The man gave Xander a parting look before being escorted into the hallway. Donovan was the last to leave. He smirked at Xander and then he was gone.

* * *

Back in the safehouse, Serena, Nicks, Tennyson, and Becky were gathered around a computer, while Adele guarded Hawk and Talon, keeping her rifle trained on them. Both men had their wrists bound behind them with zip ties.

Xander's voice came over a handheld radio sitting on the console.

"Pandora's Box is secure."

Serena grabbed the radio and moved away from the rest of the group. She spoke quietly so the others couldn't hear. "You gave it back to Marke, didn't you?"

"It's what Gibbons would have wanted."

DETROIT METROPOLITAN AIRPORT

A convoy of SUVs drove across the tarmac toward the waiting Globemaster. They pulled up to the plane, and Donovan got out of the first SUV, bringing Xiang with him. Marke followed, and then the other members of the NSA team disembarked, and everyone walked up the ramp into the plane. A few moments after that, Xander came riding up on a "borrowed" motorcycle. He parked the bike, got off, and started up the ramp.

Inside the cargo bay, Xiang looked around.

"Nice place," he said. "Spacious. Expensive."

"Shut up," Donavan said. He cuffed Xiang to a metal ring on the wall.

As he walked away, Xiang said, "You have no manners."

Donovan ignored him.

Xander entered the cargo bay. "So, are we finished?"

Marke turned to look at him, but before she could say anything her phone went off. The ringtone was "Hail to the Chief," which gave Xander a good idea who was calling.

Marke answered right away. "Sir? Thank you, sir. Minimal casualties. Triple-X performed beyond any reasonable measure of expectation." Marke then gave Xander a look, prompted, he guessed, by something the President said. She turned her back then, listening intently. Xander waited patiently until the call ended and she put her phone away.

"Let me guess," Xander said. "That was my invite to the Oval Office."

Marke turned back around to face him. "He wanted to congratulate us. With Pandora's Box in the right hands, the world doesn't have to be afraid anymore."

"In *your* hands?" Xiang said. "I don't think so."

"I told you to shut up," Donovan snapped.

"He's right," Xander said. "Nobody's safe as long as that thing is in one piece."

Marke looked at him coldly. "Game's over, Hail Mary touchdown pass to Xander Cage, home team wins, crowd goes wild. Now do what you do best and *walk away*."

"Adele, Tennyson, Nicks, Serena… I brought these people to help you. Why do I get the feeling you're not going to give them the same offer?"

"Because you're smart," Marke said. "Disappear like you did before. No one will come looking for you."

"I can't do that. Not to say that I didn't have fun when I disappeared. You gotta follow your orders, but I gotta follow my truth."

Marke stared at him for a moment, as if truly seeing him for the first time. "Gibbons was right about you after all. Too bad."

Marke drew her 9mm and aimed it at Xander, and the NSA team followed suit.

"As of ten minutes ago, the Triple-X program was officially shuttered," she said. "All active agents are to be erased from record and considered enemies of the state."

Xander kept his gaze focused on Marke as he spoke. "Xiang, tell them what happened the last time someone threatened me."

"Which one?" Xiang asked. "The guy who got blown to pieces or the guy who caught a bullet in the face?"

"I said shut up!" Donovan yelled, swinging to train his weapon on Xiang.

Xander continued looking at Marke and smiled. It felt good to be back on the right side.

Nicks glanced out the safehouse window and saw three SUVs pull up. Armed operatives poured out of the vehicles and quickly surrounded the building.

"Just for my peace of mind, tell me something," he

said. "Are NSA extraction teams normally armed like they're invading Fallujah?"

"Not generally, no," Adele said. She handed her rifle to Tennyson. "Watch the boys." Then she joined Nicks at the window.

"In that case," Nicks said, "there's a damn good chance we're about to get assassinated."

Everyone began to panic, except Serena, who quickly and calmly started grabbing her gear, readying for war.

Becky looked like she was going to throw up. "Oh God. It's happening, isn't it? They're going to start shooting at us, aren't they?"

"Let's go!" Adele said.

Serena cut Talon and Hawk free. They all had a common enemy now.

"I thought *we* were the good guys!" Talon said.

"No," Serena said. "The good guys are coming to kill us."

"You know me," Hawk said. "Wind me up and point me in a direction."

Serena bent down and yanked open a secret door in the floor that led down into the bowels of the building. The door was flush with the floor, and if you didn't know what to look for, you wouldn't know it was there.

"This shit is getting real, isn't it?" Becky said. "What do we do?"

"Be where the bullets aren't," Serena said.

They quickly entered the escape tunnel, and Serena closed the door behind them and locked it from the inside. As they climbed down a metal ladder, she took out the phone Xander had given her in case of emergency. She was pretty sure their current situation qualified. She pressed nine, just as Xander had instructed her to do, and waited for someone to answer.

Marke kept her gun trained on Xander, her hand unwavering.

"Sadly, the terrorist activated Pandora's Box one last time before we could stop him," she said. "You and your entire team were lost in the blast, along with the device itself. If the world thinks Pandora's Box is gone, then they'll never know we're using it to spy on them."

"So you're just another tyrant," Xander said.

"No. *Patriot.*"

"No," Xander said, baiting her. "*Pathetic.*"

Marke smiled grimly. "Let me educate you on the difference."

She fired point blank three times, and Xander dropped.

9

"Xander!" Xiang shouted. "Xander Cage!"

Marke walked up to Xander's prone body to make sure he was really down for the count. He lay there, unmoving, not breathing.

"They say it's the last great adventure, Cage," she said. "Be sure to send a postcard." She turned to Donovan. "Clean this shit up. Engines hot, wheels up in two!"

"Take care of it, boys," Donovan told his team, and then he followed Marke up the stairs to the Command Center. The NSA operatives busied themselves with preparing for take-off and spread throughout the cargo bay to attend to various tasks.

When everyone was out of earshot, Xander drew in a gasping breath.

"Damn, Becky," he said softly, "that's some body armor. What a rush, like skinny-dipping at the North Pole."

Xander lay only a few feet from where Xiang was cuffed, so while Xiang could see that Xander was unharmed, none of the NSA operatives—most of whom had gone into the bay's weapons cage—had noticed. Xiang grinned and spoke in a near-whisper. "You really do live for this shit, huh?"

One of Donovan's team members was working close by. Xander gave Xiang a wink and then closed his eyes. Xiang got the message.

"Hey," Xiang shouted to the operative, "I told you you had no manners."

The man turned to look at Xiang, clearly irritated. He walked over to where Xiang was cuffed, flexing his hands, eager to force Xiang to shut his mouth. When he was close enough, Xiang said, "Your mother ever teach you to zip up your pants?"

The man fell for it. He looked down at his crotch just as Xiang kicked him in the balls. The man's eyes bugged out, and he fell to the ground. Xander caught the man before he could hit and punched him in the face, rendering him unconscious. Xander lowered him to the floor and began patting his pockets.

"Come on, get me out of this shit," Xiang said.

Xander found the operative's keys, removed them from his pocket, and held them tight in his hand so they wouldn't jingle. He rose to his feet and motioned for Xiang to be quiet so he wouldn't alert the other men working in the hold. So far they hadn't noticed what had happened to their teammate, but Xander knew that wouldn't last long. He went to Xiang, hoping the NSA monkeys all carried a generic handcuff key. They did. Xander found it and freed Xiang. He then took out his phone and made a quiet call as he felt the Globemaster begin to roll down the runway.

Serena and the others managed to escape the safehouse through the secret tunnel, emerging in the multilevel electrical substation next door. The facility appeared empty, but that was no surprise. Generally substations were supervised and controlled remotely. *A perfect place for an escape tunnel to lead to,* she thought. *No one around to see you emerge from a hidden tunnel.*

They peered through one of the windows on this level and saw the NSA operatives. The team was evidently unaware of the tunnel because they continued to guard the safehouse.

"What do we do now?" Nicks said. "We don't have a ride, and if we try to leave on foot, those guys'll spot us for sure and start shooting."

Serena was trying to think of a plan where the NSA operatives finally got wise to what had happened. Maybe one of the assassins had seen them looking through the window, or maybe they'd finally remembered that safehouses were equipped with escape routes. Whatever the reason, the operatives regrouped and started coming toward the substation.

"Get away from the windows!" Serena warned.

Everyone drew back just as the NSA operatives began firing. Bullets shattered windows, sending glass shards flying.

Before any of them could return fire, Serena's phone rang, and she answered it.

"Yeah?"

"Serena, you there?" It was Xander.

"We're a little busy right now."

"Marke's got Pandora's Box and you're all loose ends," he said. *"She's gonna drop a satellite right on top of you."*

Serena quickly relayed the news to the rest of the team.

"Not if I jam the signal!" Becky said. She'd brought a duffle bag filled with goodies from her lab back on the Globemaster, and she removed a device that looked like a cell phone with external wiring and something that looked like a tuning fork protruding from the top. She pressed a button and the device activated with a soft humming sound.

"Becky's gonna jam the signal," Serena told Xander.

"What's the device's range?" he asked.

Serena relayed the question to Becky.

"Straight up?" Becky said. "Fifty thousand feet."

Serena gave Xander the information.

"Okay, then I'll keep the plane low," he said. He disconnected and Serena put the phone away.

The assassins were keeping the pressure up, continuing to fire through the windows. The bullets kept the team pinned down on one side of the level, but so far none of them had been injured.

"I need a power source to make this work," Becky said.

Serena pointed to the other side of the level. "There's a generator of some sort over there, isn't there?"

Becky glanced at where Serena pointed.

"Then go!"

Becky's eyes widened. "Me? Over there? By myself?

"Go!" Serena repeated. "*Now!*"

Becky swallowed, working up her courage. "Okay, okay, okay, I'm going!"

But before Becky could make her move, a wall exploded as an SUV slammed into it from the other side. The vehicle struck with such force that it broke through the wall and roared into the substation. The SUV came to a screeching halt and NSA operatives opened the doors, hopped out, firing.

"Cover me!" Becky shouted. She grabbed her duffle bag and started running toward the generator.

Serena and the others opened fire on the assassins while Becky reached the generator and started working on patching the signal jammer into it. The NSA operatives likely had no idea what Marke was planning or else they would've gotten the fuck out of here long before now.

Come on, Becky, she thought, *work fast!*

* * *

Once Xiang was free, he and Xander quickly worked out a plan. Xander would head up to the Command Center to deal with Marke and Donovan, while Xiang would take out the operatives and soldiers working in the cargo bay's weapons cage. Xander gave Xiang a fist bump, then he headed for the stairs as Xiang moved silently forward. Xander wished he could stick around and watch Xiang kick everyone's asses. The fight would be epic!

"I thought Xander Cage was supposed to be this incredible badass," Donovan said as he passed by her on his way to the cockpit, carrying a metal box. "Three bullets, that's all it takes?"

Marke ignored him, and Donovan continued to the cockpit. She was trying to get a signal on Pandora's Box, and she was having trouble. Frustrated, she went over to a tech working on a console. "Are you getting this interference?"

Before the tech could answer, Xander came crashing through the door. The tech stood up—whether to attack Xander or make a run for it, Xander didn't know—and he grabbed the man and slammed him into the console. Sparks flew from the damaged equipment, and when Xander let go of the man, he slid to the floor, unconscious. Marke had lunged backward when Xander took out the tech, and she bumped into another console, hitting it hard enough to make her lose her grip on Pandora's Box. The device fell to the floor and skittered away.

Xander started forward, intending to grab the device, but Donovan stepped out of the cockpit He'd put on the Exo-Gloves, and he activated them now. He gave Xander a wolfish grin.

Exo-Gloves humming with power, Donovan charged toward Xander, eyes shining with bloodlust.

Xander ran toward him, diving into a slide and using his arm to flip Donavan. He hit the ground hard.

Slamming his fists, Donovan threw Xander a furious look.

"You shouldn't have done that."

More NSA operatives entered the substation, coming through the hole in the wall made by the SUV and adding their bullets to those of their associates. Now that they were being attacked on two fronts, the team had no choice but to split up and seek cover. Nicks went with Tennyson, Talon with Hawk, and Serena and Adele joined Becky at the generator.

Becky was working feverishly to integrate the signal jammer into the machine and link her laptop to the device, using various tools from her duffle bag. But the work was proceeding slowly.

"Becky needs more time!" Serena called out.

Several assassins came their way, and Serena and Adele held them off as Becky hunkered down and kept working, bullets ripping all around her. The woman kept making little bleating sounds, almost like a frightened goat, but regardless of how terrified she was to be in the middle of her first firefight, she never stopped working. Serena was impressed by the woman's hidden reserve of strength. *We'll make a badass out of you yet,* she thought, and kept firing.

Adele, using a handgun instead of her rifle, mowed down two operatives heading for the generator as Serena shot a man approaching from a different angle. There was a catwalk around the next level up, and Serena saw an agent standing there, aiming right for her. She spun left and shot him and as he fell to his death, she spun back around and took out two more shooters on the upper level to her right.

Nicks and Tennyson crouched in a corridor entrance, one on either side, using the corners of the walls for cover. A half-dozen dead agents lay on the floor not far from where they were. Nicks thought he saw one move, and he tried to fire his 9mm at the guy, but it clicked empty. The man remained still, and Nicks decided it had only been his imagination.

"Tennyson, I need a mag!" he called out.

"For God's sake!" Tennyson reached into his pocket, grabbed hold of a clip, and tossed it to Nicks. The man reloaded, whirled around, and shot an NSA agent who was about to fire on Tennyson from the other end of the corridor. The agent went down, and Nicks drew in a shaky breath.

"Too much firepower against us!" he said.

Tennyson grew quiet, and he looked out at the dead operatives. Nicks saw where he was looking: at an ammo bag slung over the shoulder of one of the corpses.

Tennyson turned to Nicks and grinned. He threw his gun down, took out his mouth guard, and put it in.

"I've got a plan!"

Nicks realized with horror what his friend was about to do. "No!" he shouted, but it was too late. Tennyson ran out of the corridor and headed for the ammo bag. Agents on the upper-level catwalk began firing at him, and just as Tennyson reached the bag, a bullet struck his right leg, and he fell forward. Nicks didn't think. He charged out into the open, firing up at the men on the catwalk. He made it to Tennyson, grabbed hold of the man's wrist, and dragged him back toward the corridor, firing at their enemies all the way while they fired back. Bullets whizzed past him, but he gave them no thought. All he cared about was getting Tennyson to safety.

When they made it into the corridor, Nicks dragged Tennyson close to the wall, and then checked to make sure he hadn't been hit anywhere else. It looked like he was okay, all things considered. Tennyson had managed to grab hold of the ammo bag, and he clutched it to his chest, his face scrunched up in pain.

"From now on, *I* plan, *you* execute," Nicks said. "Got that?"

Tennyson's only reply was, "Ow!"

"Let's get out of here." Nicks helped his friend to stand, and he supported him as they made their way toward the opposite end of the corridor.

Adele ran out of ammo as a trio of agents closed in on her. She threw down the useless weapon and looked at the two men.

"Really? I thought we were friends."

Before either could react, she ducked around a corner and drew her hunting knife. No way in hell was she going to go down without a fight.

"Leave it to these assholes to bring guns to a knife fight," she said softly to herself.

As the first operative rounded the corner, Adele rammed the blade into his neck and yanked it free. The man cried out as his blood sprayed the wall, and she grabbed hold of his arm and tossed him aside. He fell to the floor, where she knew he'd bleed out within seconds. The next two agents had heard their companion's cry, and they came around the corridor, guns up and ready to fire. No way was she going to be able to take them both on armed with just a blade, so she turned and began running in the opposite direction, keeping her head down to avoid having it shot off.

She heard a gun blast, and she thought that was it, that her part in this battle was over. She wasn't sad. She'd lived life her way, and she had no complaints. Her only regret was that she wasn't going to be able to help Xander see this mission through to the end. *I hope Serena takes good care of you, big guy.*

But when she looked up, she saw Serena standing in the corridor in front of her, holding the Glock that she'd given her. Adele realized then that the shot she'd heard had come from *ahead* of her, not behind. Serena had just shot one of the men chasing her! Realizing that she was in the way of Serena's next shot, she hit the ground and slid forward, and Serena fired again, taking down the last agent.

As Adele got to her feet, Serena ran to the dead agent, and disarmed him. He had two pistols—one in his hand, one in a holster—and she took both. Adele sheathed her knife, and when she joined Serena, the woman tried to give the Glock back to her, but Adele took one of the agent's weapons instead.

Serena smiled at her. "Everyone needs backup, right?"

Adele returned the smile. "Guess so."

Before the two women could say anything else, more agents entered the corridor, coming from both directions now. Adele and Serena started firing, each in opposite directions, weaving and spinning to avoid being shot, performing an elaborate dance of gunfire and bloodshed as they took down one agent after another. And still more came.

Adele saw another pistol tucked in the back of Serena's pants, and she grabbed hold of it. Now both women had two guns each, and they pressed their backs together, pointed their weapons at both ends of the corridor, and unleashed a hailstorm of bullets upon the oncoming agents. They fired until all four weapons were empty, and then they lowered their arms. Dead agents filled both sides of the corridor, and there were no more in sight.

Adele allowed herself to think that maybe it was over. Until, of course, a whole new set of the assholes came running toward them from one end of the corridor. Without any ammo, the women had no choice. They turned in the opposite direction and hauled ass out of there.

Becky finally managed to get the signal jammer hooked up to the generator, *and* she'd connected her laptop to the device. As near as she could tell, everything was functioning perfectly: the generator was generating, the jammer was jamming, and the computer was computing. Of course, she'd need to do a few tests before she knew for certain that—

She heard the scuff of a boot, and she turned to see one of the NSA agents staggering toward her. The man carried a submachine gun, and at first she thought he was going to kill her, but his chest was riddled with bullet holes and blood ran from the corner of his mouth. She saw that he'd left a long blood trail behind him as she'd walked, and she realized that he'd been walking aimlessly after having been severely wounded. He probably wasn't even aware of her presence.

But then the man made a strangled noise in his throat, blood gushed from his mouth, his eyes rolled white, and he collapsed to the floor, dead. He lost his grip on his weapon when he fell, and Becky—freaked the hell out to see someone die right in front of her—snatched up the submachine gun and moved away from the generator, looking for cover.

"Guys," she called out in a half-whisper. "Where are you? Who's covering me?" When she received no answer, she muttered, "Shit!"

She was living her worst nightmare. Despite her better judgment, she'd agreed to come out into the field instead of remaining in the Globemaster's comfortable and oh-so-safe Command Center, and now here she was—wandering around a substation alone, dead people everywhere, and live ones still skulking about, looking to kill her and her friends. All she wanted to do now was find a place to hide and wait for this whole thing to—

She turned a corner and saw an NSA gunman stealthily approaching her. With no other choice, she closed her eyes, pointed the barrel of the submachine gun in his general direction, and squeezed the trigger. She knew how guns worked, of course, but. she had never actually fired one herself. She was shocked by the way the gun came alive in her hands, by the sheer *power* it radiated. The sensation was so overwhelming that she stopped firing immediately, unsure if she could handle any more of it. She opened her eyes then and saw the man she'd fired at lying on the floor, dead—and then some.

For a moment all she could do was stare at the man's corpse. *I did that,* she thought. *I killed him.* She felt sick, but she also felt—not good, exactly, but in a strange way relieved. She'd just proved that she could take care of herself in a combat situation, that she was more than just a computer nerd behind a pair of owlish glasses. She could kick ass when she had to, and kick it *hard.* She wondered if she could get people to start calling her the Techinator.

Two more gunmen came toward her then, but she wasn't worried. She could handle them. She stepped forward, intending to fire on, but she tripped clumsily and fell, losing her grip on the submachine. It hit the floor and started firing on its own, spraying the corridor with bullets. The two new gunmen jerked and jittered as their bodies were shredded by gunfire, then the machine gun went silent and fell onto its side, and the two very dead agents did likewise.

Lying on the floor, Becky stared at her second and third kills.

"Oh my God, that was *fucking awesome!*" she said, and then—forgetting she was alone—she said, "Did you guys see—"

She broke off when she saw a shitload of fresh agents approaching.

"Shit," she said, scrambling to her feet and running for cover in the opposite direction.

Xander performed a backflip, his right knee landing square on Donovan's back. But Donovan pressed his Exo-Gloves against one of the data consoles and as the gloves shattered its surface, the recoil shoved his body backwards, sending Xander flying into a corner filled with monitors.

Xander got to his feet as Donovan came at him, Exo-Gloves ratcheting like a pair of piledrivers. Xander knew he couldn't allow Donovan to land a single blow with those damn gloves. With the amount of force those things could deliver, one punch in the right place could easily prove fatal. Donovan came at him swinging, but the gloves were heavy, and that slowed his punches down a little, giving Xander more opportunity to evade them. Donovan swung at Xander over and over, but Xander kept moving, and the Exo-Gloves smashed into various pieces of tech in the Command Center, shattering plastic and sending sparks flying.

Xander fell back into one of the workstation chairs.

The chairs could swivel, but they were bolted down to prevent any unwanted movement during flight. He grinned at Donovan to goad him, and as the man moved in for the kill, Xander slipped out of the chair. Donovan slammed a glove into the chair, tearing it free from the floor and sending it flying into Marke, who was in the process of reaching for Pandora's Box. The impact knocked the woman down, but Donovan didn't seem to notice, or if he did, he didn't care. All he wanted was Xander's head on a plate.

The man bellowed in fury and charged Xander once more.

Xiang ran across the cargo bay and leaped feet first into a soldier near the doorway, drop-kicking him in the chest and sending him backwards into another man, causing them both to topple to the ground and clearing a path for him to enter the weapons cage.

Once inside, Xiang immediately turned to the soldier nearest the entrance. He broke the man's arm with a single motion, then punched him hard across the face, sending him spinning out and dropping easily. He turned to his next targets—a pair of soldiers who stood gaping at him, unable to believe how swiftly he moved. He smiled and pointed at them, as if to say, *You guys are next.* Then he spin-kicked toward them, easily knocking them down.

A fourth man stepped forward from the corner of the

cage, wielding a semi-automatic rifle he'd grabbed from a weapons rack. He aimed the weapon at Xiang, but Xiang grabbed hold of the barrel just before the man fired. He jerked the barrel a foot to the right, and when the rifle went off, the spray caught the man whose arm Xiang had broken as the man was struggling to rise to his feet. He went down and would never get up again. Xiang then shoved the barrel to the left, smashing it into the face of one of the men he'd spin-kicked as he tried to rise. His partner was trying to get up too, but Xiang struck him with a brutal neck punch, and both men fell once more. Xiang then tore the weapon from the rifleman's hand, spun it around, and rammed the butt of the gun into his face. The man dropped like a rock.

Xiang tossed the rifle aside as the first two men he'd attacked recovered and came at him from behind. Both men had grabbed semi-autos, and Xiang turned around and intercepted one's gun barrel, giving it a hard yank and flinging the man into a steel table behind him. The second man rushed toward him, but Xiang delivered a blow that sent him back down. Xiang turned and delivered a head-kick to the man on the table, knocking him onto the floor next to his friend, who was fighting to rise to his feet. Xiang pin-kicked the man's head against the edge of the steel table, and this time when the man fell, he didn't get back up.

There was a heavy metal case on the table, and Xiang

snatched it up in time to ram it into the head of the man who'd caught the rifle barrel in the face earlier. He fell once more, but then the man he'd neck punched was coming at him, but another quick strike sent him back down to the floor. The man who Xiang had hit with the rifle butt was up and made another go at him, and as Xiang dealt with that man, the one who'd gotten a face full of metal case ran to the gun rack by the doorway and grabbed hold of a semi-auto. Xiang saw what the man was doing, and he said, "Come on, baby. Let's do this!"

Xiang dropped the metal case, ran toward the man at the gun rack, and delivered a vicious spin kick to his head, sending him flying out of the cage and onto the deck outside. One of the men had retrieved the semi-auto that had fallen on the floor earlier, and now he stood up and fired two shots. Xiang leaped out of the way, rolling over two of the unconscious soldiers as the man with the rifle and the man at the gun rack—who'd gotten to his feet and snagged his own weapon—advanced on Xiang. Xiang grabbed one of the unconscious men, picked him up, and then shoved him at the two armed soldiers, knocking them down. One of them hit the floor, but the other slipped forward into the splits, so Xiang hooked his foot around the man's head and yanked, causing the man to strike the floor face-first. His gun skittered away from his hand, and Xiang stopped the weapon with his foot, slid it toward him, and using both feet, he flipped it into the air and caught it in his right hand.

One of the men on the floor started to come to. He lifted his gun, but Xiang shot it out of his hand before he could fire. Xiang stepped toward the soldier, whose hand was now bleeding, and placed the barrel of his weapon against the man's nose, scolding him with a wag of his finger. He then angled the gun barrel to the side, leaned down, and punched him in the face, returning him to unconsciousness.

Xiang left the weapons cage and returned to the main cargo bay. He headed for the stairwell that led to the upper deck, but another soldier came rushing down it, 9mm in hand. He couldn't see Xiang from the angle where he was standing, and Xiang shot the man in the back of the leg, causing him to tumble the rest of the way down the stairs. Xiang moved around to the front of the stairs to deal with the newcomer, when suddenly the Globemaster began to shake violently.

What the fuck are you doing up there, Cage? Xiang thought as he fought to maintain his balance.

Donovan grabbed hold of Xander and flung him against a console. Xander lunged forward, grabbed Donovan from above and elbowed him in the back. Just then the co-pilot ran out of the cockpit, pistol in hand, ready to fire on Xander. But Xander spun Donovan toward the co-pilot and shoved him forward. The Exo-Gloves rammed into the man, smashing him against the hull. His gun hand slammed against the wall, the weapon pointing toward the cockpit. The co-pilot's finger tightened reflexively on the trigger, the gun went off— *bam, bam, bam!*—and the bullets flew into the cockpit, each one striking the pilot.

Marke had stood pressed into a corner all this time, trying like hell to stay out of the fight. She looked to the cockpit, realized what had just happened, and her face went white with fear.

The tech Xander knocked out earlier came to, rose unsteadily to his feet and charged toward him. Xander shoved Donovan aside, grabbed onto a ceiling handhold, and swung forward to kick the man squarely in the chest. The man flew backwards, unconscious once more.

At that moment the dead pilot pitched forward onto the Globemaster's controls, throwing the plane into a steep dive. Xander, Donovan, Marke, and the unconscious tech flew upward and hit the ceiling, and then the Globemaster went into a violent spin, throwing them around the Command Center, until they hit zero gravity. Everyone now floated, and Xander and Donovan struggled to get command of their bodies so they could continue their fight. Pandora's Box floated like everything else that was loose, and Marke tried to push herself toward it, but without anything to push against, she went nowhere.

And the Globemaster continued its screaming dive toward the ground.

The zero gravity effect struck the entire plane, and in the cargo bay, Xiang, the fallen soldiers, and their weapons began floating upward. Xiang used his feet to push off the stair railing and glide toward one of the semiautomatic rifles. One of the men closed in behind Xiang, and Xiang kicked him, sending him flying toward the back of the cargo bay. The momentum caused by Xiang's kick sent him gliding toward the gun, but the man with the wounded leg was heading for it too, hands outstretched. But Xiang was moving faster, and he beat the man to the weapon. He grabbed hold of it, aimed, and finished the man off at close range.

The gun's propulsion sent Xiang flying backward, and Xiang began shooting at the surviving NSA operatives, somersaulting upside down and backwards as the rifle fired. The soldier who'd first closed in on Xiang tried to unholster his sidearm, and Xiang—still upside down— shot the man dead. He then finished his somersault and landed upright. Two more operatives still lived, and Xiang fired at them. The men fired back, but they were unable to match Xiang's acrobatic moves as he somersaulted to the rear left side of the cargo bay, ducking bullets before firing back at the two surviving operatives and pushing off the wall and down onto the floor, using it for momentum to push himself back in the air, where he fired two more times, delivering the final death blows to his last two foes.

With the Globemaster still in zero G, Xander hung from the ceiling handhold. The co-pilot had recovered, and he aimed his gun at Xander while Donovan continued to struggle with the zero gravity. The Exo-Gloves didn't help. Every time he tried to grab hold of something, the gloves activated and destroyed it. Xander saw that a pair of NSA soldiers had managed to reach the Command Center, and one of them took a shot at him.

Xander flipped down onto the floor and launched himself toward one of the men, grabbing him and using him as a human shield against the co-pilot's gunfire. The soldier stiffened as he took a bullet in the back. Xander spotted an oxygen tank mounted between two consoles. Continuing to hold onto the dead soldier, he pulled the tank free, stuffed it under the soldier's belt, broke the seal, and using the escaping oxygen as propulsion, he aimed the dead man at the co-pilot and released him.

Xander saw the dead man's Beretta floating above, and he reached up to take hold of it just as the second soldier flew toward him. The man grabbed him from behind, and his momentum sent them both floating toward the Command Center's rear door. Xander straightened, and when his feet came in contact with the door, he used it as leverage to kick backwards, sending them both down to the floor, with Xander on top. Xander rolled off the soldier and fired the Beretta at the co-pilot. The man was struggling to shove aside the dead soldier Xander had sent flying at him, and since Xander didn't have a straight shot, he banked the bullet off one of Donovan's Exo-Gloves. The bullet sparked as it ricocheted off the glove's metal and struck the co-pilot in the heart, killing him instantly. Xander then flipped himself over to shoot the soldier behind him.

The Beretta was empty, and Xander tossed the gun into the air, and launched himself toward Donovan, tackling him. Donovan in turn spun Xander into the cockpit, but not before Xander saw Marke finally snatch Pandora's Box out of the air and begin making her way toward the rear of the Command Center.

10

Hawk and Talon had taken cover behind two different stone pillars on the substation's ground level. There were NSA operatives everywhere, and Talon was out of bullets. He signaled to Hawk that he didn't have any more ammo, but Hawk just shrugged.

"We don't need any bullets," he said.

He leaned out from behind his pillar and took aim at a gas cylinder situated among a collection of equipment sitting against a nearby wall. He fired the last of his own bullets at the cylinder, causing it to ignite. The resulting explosion sent several operatives flying. Grinning in satisfaction, Hawk pulled back behind his pillar and gave Talon a nod. The other man nodded back, Hawk cast aside his weapon, and they simultaneously stepped out from behind their pillars, ready to face their enemies head-on.

Talon came out kicking, easily taking down three operatives. He rolled into a cartwheel, snapping up one of their guns lying on the floor, firing it at an agent and taking him down. He then tossed the gun into the air, hitting another operative in the head and knocking him out.

At the same time, Hawk picked up a crowbar that had been stored in the equipment stash and was sent flying when the gas cylinder exploded. The metal was still hot, but Hawk ignored it. He advanced toward an operative and swung the crowbar, knocking a gun out of the man's hand. Hawk then threw the crowbar at a group of advancing operatives, hitting one of them in the head and knocking him out. The others started shooting wildly, missing Hawk but striking an electrical wire that hung from the ceiling, fraying it incrementally.

Hawk spin-kicked, headbutted, and dropkicked multiple NSA men. He disarmed one operative by grabbing the gun out of his holster and slamming him face-first into the floor. Hawk was surprised to see water splash into the air when the man's face hit, and he glanced over toward the area where the cylinder had exploded and saw that the blast had taken out a chunk of wall and ruptured a water pipe. Water was gushing from the broken pipe and spreading across the floor.

Spotting a shit-ton more operatives coming toward them, Hawk rolled himself in Talon's direction, getting his clothes wet in the process. He grabbed a machine gun along the way and sprayed an operative with gunfire, taking him down. He saw Talon launch into a run then, and he tossed the gun away, got to his feet, just in time to give Talon a boost, becoming a human springboard for the man. Talon soared toward the now-sparking electrical wire, and once Hawk realized what he intended to do, he hauled ass to get away from the wet part of the floor. Talon flipped over the wire, and as he did, he grabbed hold of the wire, yanked it apart, released it, and continued onward. The two ends of the live wire touched the floor, and more importantly, the water *covering* the floor—water the operatives were standing in. Electricity popped and crackled, surging through the operatives' bodies, frying them from the inside out.

Talon landed beyond the wet section of floor, rolled, and came up on his feet. He grabbed a machine gun that an operative had dropped, then he ran toward Hawk, making sure to give the water a wide berth. Hawk also retrieved a fallen weapon, and the two men ran off in search of their companions.

Tennyson, Becky, and Nicks hid behind a concrete pillar, hunkered down, out of bullets, out of space, as NSA operatives closed in on them. Serena and Adele hid behind the next pillar over. They checked their weapons, but they were also out of ammo. They tossed their guns aside, and Adele offered Serena a knife. Serena took it with a grateful smile.

Hawk and Talon ran up and took positions behind the pillar next to Serena and Adele's. They'd had to fight their way here, and they checked their weapons to see if they had any ammo left.

"You got anything?" Hawk asked Talon.

Talon shook his head. "Nothing."

"Me neither," Hawk said, mad enough to spit.

They looked to Serena and Adele, both of whom were now armed only with knives. It looked like Nicks, Tennyson, and Becky didn't even have that much to fight with.

Serena held up three fingers, her message clear. She intended for them to storm the remaining operatives. It would be a suicide run, of course, but what else could they do? Attack, don't attack... either way they'd die. At least Serena's way, they had a chance—however slim—of taking some of the motherfuckers with them.

"We go in three," Hawk said to Talon, and Talon nodded.

One of Tennyson's pant legs was soaked with blood, but Nicks and Becky helped him stand. Tennyson might be wounded, but he wasn't going to sit this one out.

Three.

Serena lowered one of her fingers.

Two.

She lowered the next.

One.

But just as the team started to make a move to storm the waiting attackers, a huge explosion sent operatives flying to their deaths all around them. Confused, everyone looked up to see a bearded African-American man in a black leather jacket standing on the upper level catwalk, holding a large grenade launcher. He shouldered the weapon once more, and launched another grenade. This one exploded in the midst of operatives close to Becky, Tennyson, and Nicks. A third blast took out more operatives near Hawk and Talon.

The newcomer saw a dozen more operatives coming in through the opening in the substation's wall. Reinforcements. He took aim at the SUV parked near the opening and fired. The vehicle exploded, becoming an inferno that engulfed the recently arrived operatives, killing them all. Game over.

As the dust settled, the team moved out from behind the pillars, surveying the carnage. A voice called out from above them then.

"Whassup?" their savior said.

Becky grinned. "Darius Stone," she said. "Triple-X since 2005."

Serena was going to have to find a *very* special way to show Xander her gratitude for giving her that phone. "Thanks for the assist," she said to Darius.

"X takes care of its own," Darius said.

Everyone smiled until Becky's eyes widened as she had a sudden realization.

"Oh my god," she said.

Serena did *not* like the sound of that.

Xander grabbed Donovan from behind, got him in a chokehold, and then pulled him back into the bathroom between the Command Center and the cockpit. The door slammed closed behind them, and Donovan tried to use his Exo-Gloves on Xander, but while the gears whirred and the pistons snapped, he couldn't turn in this small space. Unable to break free from Xander's grip, Donovan punched the bathroom mirror in front of him, sending glass shards flying everywhere. The force of the punch dislodged Xander's grip and shoved him back into wall and down onto the toilet, his legs akimbo in zero gravity, glass fragments floating around him like sharp-edged snow.

With Xander off his back, Donovan could turn, so he did so and faced Xander.

"What's wrong, hotshot?" Donovan said, a smug smile on his face. "No witty comeback? No clever one-liner?"

"Nah," Xander said. "Just finally worked out that math problem."

Donovan's features twisted into a mask of fury, and he drew back his arm, and punched an Exo-Glove toward Xander. But Xander rolled away before the high-tech weapon could strike him, and Donovan ended up hitting the toilet. The force of the punch sent the toilet down through the plane, leaving a gaping hole. Air rushed out as the cabin depressurized, causing a near-deafening roaring sound.

Xander grabbed hold of the door as the wind tore at him. Donovan tried to grab onto the sink, but it shattered beneath the force of the still-ratcheting Exo-Gloves. He kicked Donovan back toward the opening where the toilet had been, and the man was pulled toward it. As he was sucked in, he desperately reached out with the Exo-Glove and tried to get a grip on the bathroom walls. Xander kicked the man in the chest, and the impact was too much. Donovan was pulled through the opening and disappeared.

"That's gonna take a second flush," Xander said.

Darius stood with the others while Becky sat on the floor next to the power generator and checked the data readout on her laptop. It took her only a few seconds to review the information sent by the signal jammer, and when she was finished, she looked up at them with an expression of sheer horror.

"We failed," she said.

Xander floated into the cockpit, reached past the dead pilot, grabbed the shift mechanism and, after some struggle, righted the Globemaster, taking it out of zero G.

His body suddenly felt heavy again as he felt the effects of gravity settled on him, but as much fun as it had been to fly around weightless, he preferred to defy gravity the old-fashioned way: on the back of a motorcycle or free-climbing up a sheer rock face. He removed the pilot from his seat and laid him gently on the floor. Then he took the seat and examined the control console. He'd never flown a plane this complex before, but how hard could it be?

He wanted to at least set the autopilot so he could go look for Marke, but before he could touch any of the controls, his phone rang. He answered it, knowing there was only one person who would be calling him now.

Serena didn't waste words. *"She did it. She activated Pandora's Box before we could stop her."*

Xander looked through the cockpit window and pictured the satellite—or what was left of it after reentry—falling toward Earth, a fiery missile of death on a collision course with Detroit. And although Marke had aimed it at Serena and the others, the building they were in was located downtown. The force of the satellite's impact would devastate the surrounding area, resulting in who knew how many deaths.

"Lucky for us I got something to knock it out of the sky," he said.

Serena was silent for a moment, and then she said, *"It's a one in a million…"*

"Give me the co-ords," he said.

She did so, somewhat reluctantly, he thought, and he typed them into the Globemaster's navigation system: 42.3314N, 83.0458W.

He couldn't bring himself to say goodbye to her, so he disconnected and put his phone back in his pocket. *Time to do some flying,* he thought. He gripped the plane's yoke, took a deep breath, and started ascending toward the rapidly falling satellite.

Xiang dropped back to the cargo bay floor as normal gravity was restored. Bodies of dead NSA soldiers lay scattered around him, and he looked around to make sure that he'd gotten them all. The last thing he wanted was for some motherfucker that he missed to sneak up on him and—

A shot rang out and a bullet slammed into his leg.

He looked up in the direction the shot had come from and saw Marke standing at the top of the stairs, pistol in hand. He tried firing back, but the semi-auto he held was out of ammo. His leg was a blaze of agony, and he stumbled into the side of a bulkhead and used it to prop himself up.

"You've *got* to be kidding!" He threw the rifle away in disgust.

As Marke began to make her way down the stairs, Xiang turned away and hit the button to open the cargo bay door. Wind rushed in through the cargo bay, but both he and Marke were far enough away from the door that the wind had little effect on them.

Marke surveyed the carnage as she reached the bottom of the stairs. If she felt anything on seeing so many of her people dead, she didn't show it. She stepped toward Xiang, keeping her gun trained on him, but she didn't get too close. The woman wasn't stupid.

She held up Pandora's Box with her other hand. "With this, we're going to change the world. You gonna help me get out of here?"

"No," Xiang said. "Your world's not the world I wanna live in."

The period of zero gravity had caused all kinds of equipment to float around the cargo bay, but once normal gravity was restored, everything fell, and now shit was scattered all over the place. A parachute pack had fallen nearby, and it gave Xiang an idea.

"Yes," he said.

"Yes, what?" Marke replied.

"Today's your day."

Despite his injured leg, Xiang moved with lightning speed. He grabbed hold of the parachute and lunged toward Marke. She managed to get a shot off but missed him as he landed at her feet. He swiftly wrapped the pack's straps around her legs, and pulled the rip cord. The chute deployed, was caught by the wind, and Marke was yanked off her feet and pulled toward the open bay door.

She was so surprised, she didn't scream, didn't curse

him, didn't make a sound of any sort. She clawed at the floor, trying to find some sort of handhold, but she found none. She lost hold of Pandora's Box in doing so, and the device skittered after her. She flew down the ramp and out into the open air, Pandora's Box following a short way behind.

Xiang couldn't let the device fall out of the plane.

Sometimes being one of the good guys is a real pain in the ass, he thought.

Ignoring the pain in his wounded leg, he ran toward the bay door, snagged another parachute pack lying on the floor, and dove toward the ramp. He slid down just in time to grab hold of Pandora's Box before he fell out of the plane and began freefalling.

The air was thinning out, and it was getting damn cold inside the cockpit. Xander knew he was pushing the Globemaster to operate at altitudes it wasn't designed for—and he could say the same thing for himself—but he couldn't give up. He had to stop the satellite, no matter what happened.

Xander was beginning to feel the effects of oxygen deprivation—nausea, headache, and euphoria. At least with the euphoria, he didn't care about the other symptoms. The Globemaster was practically on the edge of space now, and the engines began to stall.

Come on, you bucket of bolts, Xander thought. *I just*

need you to hold together a little bit longer…

And then he saw the satellite ahead, the metallic object the size of a bus, wreathed in white-hot flame, trail of fire stretching out behind it. It seemed to grow larger as the Globemaster headed for it. Five hundred feet to go, Xander estimated. Four hundred. Three…

Xander jumped out of the pilot's seat and raced back through the plane just as the satellite smashed into the cockpit, the force of the impact tearing the Globemaster apart. Xander ran full out, through the Command Center, down the stairs into the cargo bay, and toward the bay door which—thankfully—was already open. As he flung himself toward the open door, the plane ripped into shreds around him, and then everything went black.

THE STRATOSPHERE

Three miles above the Earth, Xander fell. At first there was no sound, but then he broke through into the atmosphere, and the rush of air blasted his face and eardrums. But he didn't feel it because he was unconscious.

And still he fell.

Serena, Darius, and the rest of the team rushed out of the substation and looked up at the explosion high overhead. None of them said anything. What could they say? All they could do was stand, watch, and hope.

* * *

10,000 feet…

Xander, still unconscious, fell in an uncontrollable spin, the ground rushing up to meet him.

7,500 feet…

Xander's eyes remained closed.

5,000 feet…

Xander's eyes popped open. At first he was overwhelmed by the air roaring past him and the dizzying sensation of spinning. But it took only a few seconds for him to orient himself, and he turned over and spread out his arms and legs to better control his descent.

Only one tiny problem, Xander, my man, he thought. *You're still falling at fucking terminal velocity.*

Debris from the wreckage of the Globemaster whipped past him, and he scanned his surroundings, searching for something, anything that he might be able to use to save himself.

2,500 feet…

And there it was, a hundred feet below him—a cargo crate from the Globemaster, with its aerial drop chute still intact. Xander kicked off a chunk of passing debris, brought his legs together and flattened his arms against his sides and zoomed toward the crate like a rocket. He reached the crate and grabbed hold of it, fighting against the G-force.

1,000 feet…

Xander rode the crate as it plummeted toward the ground, and then he reached for the parachute and pulled the cord. The chute deployed, caught air, and Xander held on tight so the sudden jerk of the crate slowing wouldn't throw him off.

500 feet…

The crate continued slowing, but not nearly fast enough. Xander braced for impact…

An SUV raced to the impact site—a vacant lot on the edge of town that was obscured by a massive cloud of dust. The vehicle skidded to a stop on the street, and the doors popped open. Serena and all the others—including Xiang—emerged, everyone afraid of what they might find. The team stood at the curb, reluctant to go any closer.

Tennyson—leg wound bandaged—removed his fedora and held it in both hands.

"Guess he finally ran out of lives," he said sadly.

But then a silhouette appeared in the dust cloud, and Xander came walking toward them. He moved stiffly, but he was moving, and that was all that counted.

Becky grinned so wide it looked like her cheeks might crack. "Guess you haven't been paying attention," she said.

Adele raised her hand in three-fingered salute which Xander returned, tapping his heart.

He looked at Nicks. "If it ain't on video, it didn't happen. Tell me you got that."

Nicks smiled and held up a GoPro camera.

"This is some Hall of Fame shit right here, bro," he said.

Hawk and Talon stood off to the side.

"Not bad. *I* could've done that, though," Hawk said.

"Bullshit," Talon said.

Hawk scowled. "Shut up."

Xiang walked up to Xander, cigarette in his mouth. Xander noticed the man's limp. Hopefully, it wouldn't be permanent. He doubted it would be. Xiang was one tough sonofabitch.

"What happened to Marke?" Xander asked.

Xiang smiled. "The ground broke her fall." He removed Pandora's Box from his pocket and handed it to Xander.

Xander grinned. "I finally figured out who you remind me of. Me."

Xiang laughed. "Other way around, Cage. Other way around."

Xander dropped Pandora's Box onto the ground and smashed it under his foot. The team turned to walk away after that, except for Serena, who came toward him.

Xiang removed the cigarette from his mouth and flicked it away. He then took an entire pack from his pocket, tossed it to the ground, and joined the others. "Not today," he said.

Xander looked at Serena, his expression serious. "What about the debris from the crash?"

"From the reports we've gotten, a lot of it fell in the river. The rest was scattered and mostly landed outside the city. The stuff that *did* hit the city didn't do much damage, and so far it looks like there were no casualties and only minor injuries."

Xander was relieved to hear it.

He smiled at Serena then. "Still don't believe in good guys?"

She cocked her head to the side and gave him a half-smile. "It's okay if you're a *little* bad."

"How bad?" he asked.

She stepped into his arms and kissed him. The embrace lasted for several moments, but then Xander heard a car approach. The rumble of the engine sounded familiar, and he stepped away from Serena and looked over to see a purple GTO pull up to the curb. The driver parked, got out, and started walking toward them.

Darius nodded to the impact site. "That right there was a hell of an entrance," he said.

Xander nodded to the GTO. "That's a hell of a car."

"Gibbons told me to keep an eye on it. He said I'd know why when I needed to." Darius shrugged. "Now I know."

Xander and Serena held hands as the three of them walked over to the car. Xander gazed at the vehicle fondly. "It's exactly how I left it."

"I took it on a few dates," Darius said.

"X takes care of its own," Xander said. "That's why I knew you'd come through."

"To get to work with the legendary Xander Cage? Hell, yeah. Where do I sign up?"

Xander gave Darius a fist bump. "You just did."

"Now, you know you done took a piss on the wrong damn picnic," Darius said. "The whole world's gonna come after us."

Xander put his arm around Serena, and she smiled.

"Wouldn't have it any other way," he said.

Darius grinned "Yeah."

11

The choir sang a joyous rendition of "Oh Happy Day," the congregation on their feet, enthusiastically clapping along with the music. A large photo of Gibbons rested on a display easel in front of the pulpit. This might technically be a funeral, but the atmosphere was as much one of celebration as it was mourning—maybe more. *This is the way to do it right,* Xander thought. He hoped that when his time came, the people he loved would throw one hell of a party in his memory, one that would be talked about for decades afterward.

He sat on a pew in the church's upper level, watching the service from above. No one else was up here. He needed to be alone with his thoughts today, and he deeply appreciated that his friends understood and respected his desire.

He watched as Serena—wearing a lovely but tasteful black dress—entered the church and headed for the front row of pews, joining their companions: Xiang, Adele, Becky, Tennyson, Nicks, Hawk, and Talon. It struck Xander that all of them were the team Gibbons had been trying to put together from the start, and now here they were, united at last. Only one person was missing… Then Xander saw Darius—dressed in a suit and tie—enter off to the side. The man stood for a moment, taking it all in, before joining the rest of the team. All of Triple-X, together at last.

It's too bad Gibbons can't be here to see this, Xander thought.

He heard soft footsteps on the stairs as someone made their way to the upper level. He wondered who it was.

A man wearing a cap, dark glasses, and a brown leather jacket over a maroon sweater stepped onto the upper level

He grinned at Gibbons. "Now *that's* an impressive trick."

Gibbons smiled as he removed his cap. "What? You think you're the only one who knows how to play dead?" He looked upon the congregation and shook his head. "It's some pretty surreal shit being at your own funeral."

The pastor stepped up to the pulpit then and spoke into a microphone.

"We thought we'd end with Augustus's favorite song," he said.

The choir began singing "What a Wonderful World."

"I *love* this song," Gibbons said, turning to Xander. "You know, it could be a wonderful world, too, if we'd stop doin' bad shit to it."

"If you wanted me out of retirement, you could have just asked."

"No, you always responded to... less subtle motivation."

Xander chuckled. He couldn't argue with that.

"So, with you here and all that's going on, now what?" he asked.

"Continue being the rebel the world doesn't know it needs," Gibbons said. "Watch the watchers, fight the enemy from within."

"People have a seen a lot of things in me, but you're the only one who ever saw a hero," Xander said. "But it's damn complicated."

"Really? Well, let me simplify it for you: kick some ass, get the girl, and try to look dope doing it."

Xander grinned. "Okay, Gibbons. I can *definitely* make that work."

Gibbons gave Xander a parting smile, then turned and started for the stairs. Xander saw someone waiting for Gibbons in the doorway: a young man who looked an awful lot like the soccer player Neymar. It looked like Gibbons wasn't done recruiting yet.

"Junior, let's bounce," Gibbons said to Neymar, and the two men headed down the stairs.

Xander leaned back, put his hands behind his head, a big smile on his face.

"Yeah, it *is* a wonderful world."

ACKNOWLEDGEMENTS

Special thanks to my wonderful editor Natalie Laverick and to my fantastic agent Cherry Weiner. Extra-special thanks to my amazing wife Christine, who took care of everything else in our lives while I finished this book under a tight deadline. Also thanks to everyone involved in making such a fun movie!

ABOUT THE AUTHOR

Shirley Jackson Award finalist Tim Waggoner has published over thirty novels and three short-story collections of dark fiction. He teaches creative writing at Sinclair Community College and in Seton Hill University's MFA in Writing Popular Fiction program. You can find him on the web at www.timwaggoner.com.

For more fantastic fiction, author events,
competitions, limited editions and more

VISIT OUR WEBSITE
titanbooks.com

LIKE US ON FACEBOOK
facebook.com/titanbooks

FOLLOW US ON TWITTER
@TitanBooks

EMAIL US
readerfeedback@titanemail.com